ACADEMY OF THE LOST LABYRINTH

The Talismans of Time

Stephen H. Provost

Cover design by Melody Simmons
Interior images are in the public domain

Dragon Crown Books 2020, 2023

ISBN: 978-1-949971-04-0

For those who still believe.

Contents

Chapter One

Welcome

Twenty years.

That's how long Alamina had been headmistress at the Academy. It still looked much the way it always had on the outside. Ivy climbed up the three stories of its gray stone walls, which presided over expansive gardens filled with wisteria, foxglove, hydrangea, and rambling rose. Three students stood chatting in a white gazebo, at the edge of a pond filled with lily pads and an assortment of colorful carp.

The inside, of course, was far different than it had once been. It had been built as a manor house in the sixteenth century, and had served as such for generations. It was only at the end of the nineteenth century that it had been converted into a school campus, many of its bedrooms transformed into classrooms where youths ages ten to eighteen studied a diverse array of subjects.

There were the typical courses in arithmetic, from basic math to calculus; in literature and biology, in history and physics. But the Academy of the Lost Labyrinth also offered subjects that were less, shall we say, conventional. The schedule of courses posted on the bulletin board in Alamina's office included titles such as:

The Benefits and Hazards of Time Travel
Changing Shapes and Changing Back
The Circle of History
The Ethics of Dream Striding
Memory Magic
Mythology: Fact and Fiction

One of the course titles was crossed out with thick red ink and marked as CANCELED in capital letters: Navigating the Labyrinth.

The class was canceled because the labyrinth wasn't where it was supposed to be, in the gardens behind the school. It only appeared when a particular kind of student, a Pathfinder, was in need of it. At one time, as many as six Pathfinders had been enrolled at the Academy, but at present, there were none. That wasn't to say, though, that there weren't any Pathfinders on the grounds. There was at least one that Alamina knew of.

Herself.

But the labyrinth had been gone for as long as she'd been here, and she was beginning to wonder whether it would ever appear again. Whole classes of students had come and gone without ever venturing inside the Lost Labyrinth. Not that this was necessarily a bad thing: The labyrinth could be a very dangerous place.

Still, it seemed strange that it had been gone so long. The last time Alamina had seen it was when she arrived at the school to take her position.

Her arrival had hardly been inconspicuous: She had flown in from Iowa—on the wings of one dragon, accompanied by another.

At the time, she'd had no intention of becoming headmistress. She hadn't even known for sure what she would find here among the rolling hills of Yorkshire.

Who she found had surprised her even more.

At first, she hadn't even recognized the old man who met her on the front lawn; it was something in his eyes that had given him away. ...

"You haven't changed a bit," he said, smiling broadly to reveal that he still had all his teeth, even at nearly a hundred years of age. He wore a white suit, and his head was completely bald, with only a wispy ring of white hair growing above his ears and around the back. He picked up his cane, which was crowned by the wood-carved head of a crow—one of his students had personally gifted it to him on graduation—and half-fell forward as he embraced Alamina.

"You have," she said. "Changed, I mean."

"Time does that to a man," he chuckled, "unless, that is, you jump the circle."

An odd-looking cat who looked quite old sat on his shoulder, purring softly. The odd-looking thing about her was the fact that she had nine tails, each of which waved lazily as she opened her eyes about a quarter of the way.

"Oh, hello," she said. "How did you get here?"

"The dragons brought me," said Alamina, then leaned close to the man's ear and whispered. "I didn't think she'd still be alive."

"I can hear you," the cat said. "My hearing hasn't gone yet. And yes, I'm still alive. I'm on my eighth life."

Alamina smiled. "Is Ruffus...?"

"Oh, he's been gone for some time," the cat said. "Bloodhounds aren't as long-lived as we cats."

"Admit it Isis, you miss him," the man said.

The cat meowed softly, and he scratched her under her chin.

Alamina introduced him to Illian, the woman who'd ridden in on the other dragon. She remained tight-lipped, though, and simply nodded as she looked him up and down. It wasn't clear whether she failed to recognize him, or whether she thought she did and dismissed the idea because it seemed too implausible that he could be the person he seemed.

Alamina looked at him, amazed. She'd never thought she'd actually see him again. It had seemed like only yesterday he had been a young boy, shorter than she. To her, it *had* been only yesterday. To him, it had been eighty years.

"I've only jumped the circle, as you put it, once. And only just now," she said. "I'm still trying to figure this all out."

The man threw back his head and laughed. "You should have taken one of my classes. You'd be an expert by now!" He waved his cane toward the impressive mansion that had once been called Ridley Manor, but which was now a very special school for more than three-hundred very special students. Alamina noticed that a large dormitory building had been added, along with a separate library, a gymnasium, and an arched hall that ran between the dorm and the main house. "Do you like what I've done with the place?" he asked.

"I'm impressed," she said, trying not to sound too awed by it all. She'd known he was important, but she had no idea he had been destined to establish an academy. Now she knew why he'd needed to switch places with her—at least a fragment of the reason why.

But his expression turned suddenly serious, and he asked: "What are you doing here?"

"I'm not really sure."

"I may be old, Alamina," the man said, "but I can still read my calendar, and according to that calendar, you're about twenty years too early."

"I know," she answered. "But why do you keep calling me Alamina?"

"It's the name I first knew you by: your magical name. It's strange, though. My memory of that encounter between us seems to be fading—to the point I can barely recall it. It's almost as though it never happened. I just can't figure out why. My memory is the one thing I've always been able to count on. It's my gift, you know."

"I do," she said. "What do they call *you* these days?"

"To my face, they call me 'Headmaster.' Behind my back, they call me all sorts of unspeakable things. They complain I never forget anything they've done wrong—which is true. But I can't help that. I *do* have an impeccable memory." He winked. "A few of them like me, though. They call me 'the Great.'"

When he said that, she saw something strange: The man seemed to grow momentarily translucent, flickering, and fading before returning to normal again.

Alamina rubbed her eyes. "It's not just your memory that's fading."

The man nodded. "So I've been told. I'm afraid it's because you arrived early, but on the other hand, it's a good thing you're here, because I'll need someone to take over the Academy for me when I'm gone, and I can think of no one better."

"Gone? I won't let that happen!"

"I'm afraid you're too late to stop it," the headmaster said. "Besides, even if you could stop me from fading away—and I don't think you can—I'm an old man nearing the end of my days. You're still young enough to deal with these all these undisciplined ragamuffins." He laughed. "A word I picked up from Miss Owl."

Alamina smiled. She missed Miss Owl already.

"But I have no idea what it takes to run a school," she protested.

"An academy," he corrected.

"Or an academy."

"Neither did I," the headmaster said. "I only knew I did *not* want to run it the way other people run schools."

He took her inside the house and gave her a tour. Each of the classrooms had a quote inscribed over the doorframe:

"Magic is believing in yourself. If you can do that, you can make anything happen." — Johann Wolfgang van Goeth

"Do not go where the path may lead. Go instead where there is

no path, and leave a trail." — Ralph Waldo Emerson

"The distinction between past, present, and future is only a stubbornly persistent illusion." — Albert Einstein

"The chameleon changes color to match the earth; the earth doesn't change color to match the chameleon." — Senegalese proverb

"Memories are the key not to the past, but to the future." — Corrie ten Boom

"That one's my favorite," the headmaster said.

Alamina wasn't surprised.

Some of the classrooms were empty, but most were filled with children and teens, listening with varying degrees of attention to lectures, working on assignments, or conducting experiments. Her host poked his head inside one classroom to say a quick hello to the teacher, a woman of advanced years whose hair was nonetheless still bright red. She stood at the front of the class, talking about how to turn oneself into a toad without accidentally becoming a tadpole. This was important, she said, because tadpoles need to stay in the water, "and unless you're in a bathtub when you change, you might find yourself hung out to dry."

Some in the class laughed at this, although others

didn't seem to get the joke. The instructor turned her head and nodded slightly when the headmaster entered the room. Was that a twinkle in her eye? Was there something between the two of them?

Alamina shook her head and hid a smile behind her hand. It was none of her business. It just seemed odd to see him the way he was now and to think of him as having a romantic interest. He was just so... different.

The teacher turned her attention back to the class and admonished them to never, under any circumstances, take the form of an inanimate object.

"Why?" asked one of the students.

She responded with a question of her own: "What does 'inanimate' mean?"

"You can't move."

"Exactly," she said. "If you're inanimate, that means you can't move *anything*. That includes your central nervous system. All those neurons that are firing all the time in your brain? They don't fire if you're inanimate."

"Then how do we change back?" another student asked.

"You don't. That's the problem."

She followed the headmaster out of the classroom and closed the door behind her. There was noise coming from the room next door: the sound of students talking and laughing.

The headmaster stopped just outside the door and

raised a finger before opening it.

"New teacher," he whispered conspiratorially to Alamina. "He hasn't figured out how to command his students' attention yet."

As he opened the door, a paper airplane flew from a young boy's hand toward a beleaguered man in a three-piece suit who was writing something on a whiteboard. The boy's creation looped once in the air, then did a nosedive to the floor a few feet from its intended target.

"You're no Daedalus, young man," the headmaster said.

The students, who had been restless and inattentive a moment earlier, grew immediately silent and sat up straight in their chairs, eyes to the front of the class.

A girl near the front raised her hand.

"Angela," the teacher said, calling on her.

"Mr. Firpo, who's Daedalus?"

"You'd know, if you'd been paying attention," the headmaster said, his tone instructive but firm.

"Um... er... yes. Quite right," said the teacher. "Daedalus was one of the greatest craftsmen and inventors in ancient Greece. He was the first person to solve the mystery of flight." He looked down at the paper airplane. "And, of course, he built the famous labyrinth."

The headmaster led Alamina out of the room. "The mythology class is always a challenge," he said. "Half the students think they don't need to learn it, and the rest think they know more than they do. They're sure that the history is really fantasy, and vice versa. Firpo will set them straight, though. He'll be fine once he gets his feet wet," he said. Then he added: "You'll make sure of that."

"But I haven't accepted..."

He waved his hand to fend off any further objection.

Alamina didn't want to seem rude, so she tried a different tack. "What, exactly, does the position entail?"

They had come to the last classroom, the one at the end of the third-floor corridor, and found it empty. Above the door were printed the words of Thomas Paine, the American revolutionary. Instead of answering her question, he glanced up at them, and her eyes followed his.

"The inquiry ceases at once, for the time hath found us."

She looked up at them, and frowned, then back at the headmaster.

But he was gone.

Chapter Two

Field Trip

So, it had come to this. Alamina had accepted the position of headmistress because she had no idea what else to do—or where else to go.

"Time runs in a circle," she'd once been told, and it truly seemed that her life had come full circle.

Except that something had gone wrong, and she needed to right it.

Because she had time-jumped to a point on the circle that was twenty years too early, she'd had to wait those twenty years to set things right. She could have tried to jump again and find the proper landing spot. But her initial failure had affected her. What if her second try only complicated things even further? What if it created more problems than it solved? It was ironic that her own gift, which qualified her to teach a class called "Practical Time Shifting," should have been the one talent she feared invoking.

It wasn't as if she had accomplished nothing in those twenty years. She had learned how to run the Academy and had earned the trust of the teachers—most of them, anyway. The students liked her, too. The word was that they had warmed to her more easily than the old headmaster, who had spent so much of his time with his nose in old books that the pupils barely saw him. Alamina had taken a far more active role in running the school, even teaching two or three sections herself every semester, and had taken a personal interest in many of her pupils.

Not long after she arrived, they had started calling her Alamina, which she actually preferred to her given name. It was familiar to her from another time and place, and it seemed odd, but somehow fitting, that she should hear it again just now. It was a Romani name, but of Arabic origin: It meant "smart person."

She liked that, and it hadn't been long before everyone was calling her by the new name.

So, she had waited for the proper moment to arrive. Now, it was nearly here.

There was a knock at the door, and she looked up from her desk, where her pen sat poised over a sheet of paper as she lingered deep in thought.

"Come," she said.

The door opened, and a man in a long brown coat and a Fedora entered, nearly creating a breeze with his confident stride.

"Headmistress," he said, leaning over in front of her and placing two close-fisted hands on her desk, knuckles down. "We have a problem."

"Oh?" Alamina was unperturbed by his brashness.

"Three of the older students," he began. "They refuse to take instruction. Two of them have been held back twice already, and the third is so impertinent that none of the teachers can control him."

She leaned back. "Let me guess, Mr. Thorvald," she said, a thin-lipped half-smile on her face. "Joey, Vano, and Django."

Mr. Thorvald nodded once, decisively. "The gypsy boys."

"Roma," she corrected him. "Or Romani. We do *not* call them 'gypsies' in this school. Is that clear?"

Mr. Thorvald's confidence seemed to waver for a brief moment. Then he plowed ahead. "They are disrupting all their classes, poisoning the learning environment," he said. "What do *you* intend to do about it?"

A germ of an idea began to form in her head.

"Perhaps the learning environment is poisoning

them," she suggested.

Thorvald stood up straight, taking his knuckles off her desk. "I hardly think the *school* is the problem, Headmistress," he said haughtily. "If you want to blame the instructors for the students' bad behavior, you'll have a significant morale problem. And I don't need to tell you how difficult it is to find *qualified* instructors to teach here."

Alamina frowned. He was right, of course. In her twenty years as headmistress, she had found recruiting instructors one of her most challenging tasks. Time Wielders, Dream Striders, Memory Masters, and Shape Changers didn't exactly grow on trees; Pathfinders even less so. And it wasn't exactly practical to take out ads in a newspaper when you wanted to keep the true nature of your school a secret. As far as anyone on the "outside" knew, the Academy of the Lost Labyrinth was just an ordinary parochial school with the ordinary name "Ridley Institute." That name was even inscribed on a sign at the front gate and over the academy entrance to keep up appearances. When it came to filling positions, she had to rely on word of mouth, and because almost all gifted individuals preferred to keep their talents hidden, networking wasn't exactly a top priority.

She didn't need a faculty morale problem, but she didn't need a faculty revolt led by Mr. Thorvald, either.

She leaned forward, and Thorvald took an

involuntary step back.

"I am most definitely *not* blaming the instructors," she said. "But need I remind you that the first headmaster founded this academy precisely because he believed conventional forms of instruction were inadequate for students with exceptional gifts? I am not implying any shortcoming by the instructors, Mr. Thorvald, but I am also aware that we must continue to innovate, moving forward. And I need not remind you that I, myself, am a member of this faculty. As such, I have not only the right, but the responsibility, to pursue such innovations." She paused. "I do hope you approve." Her tone was more a dare than a declaration.

Thorvald frowned but nodded.

"Very well, then," she said. "I think, perhaps, a field trip is in order. Since the three students in question are in *my* class on Practical Time Shifting, I will deal with them from here. In the meantime, they are excused from all other classes and will report to my office for detention after school today."

"But..."

"Have I made myself clear?"

Thorvald contained a sigh. "You have, Headmistress."

"Very well then. Go and carry out my instructions. And if you breathe a word of complaint about them to anyone else on the faculty, I will hear about it and will arrange for your termination. Is *that* clear?"

"It is."

"Very well, then. Dismissed."

Mr. Thorvald turned on one heel and exited the room even more swiftly, but with far less confidence, than he had when he had entered.

What Alamina hadn't told Mr. Thorvald was that she had a connection to the three Romani boys that none of the newer teachers knew about: Their mother, Ethelinda, had been an instructor at the Academy when she'd first arrived, and they had formed a friendship as close as sisters. In fact, it had been Ethelinda who had bestowed the name Alamina on the headmistress.

Both of them were new at the time, and both had been separated from their families.

Like Alamina, Ethelinda was a Time Wielder. She had come to the Academy from the Black Forest in Germany, where her family had lived for generations, moving in a caravan from one place to another until they were driven out in the Nazi purges of the Second World War.

Unfortunately, her husband was captured before they could make their escape, and she never learned what had become of him.

However, she and her two sons avoided capture by the SS, the Nazi squadron charged with rounding up

Jews, Romani, Slavs and others. She used her gift to jump forward in time half a century, landing in Yorkshire with her two very young sons. There, she came to the attention of the headmaster, who brought her to work at the school shortly before he disappeared. She was expecting her third child at the time, and gave birth to a son, Django, seven months after her arrival.

But she never forgot her beloved husband, searching every day for him with the help of a crystal ball that enabled her to see across great distances.

Alamina thought she would, in time, come to terms with their separation, but Ethelinda told her that theirs had been a deep and enduring love, and each day brought her no closer to reconciling herself to his fate. Eventually, she resolved to use her gift to jump back in time and go in search of him, so she could warn him against his impending capture. She seemed confident she would ultimately return to the present day, and asked Alamina to take care of her young boys until she could do so. Each of them, like her, was gifted, and would require a proper education—the kind that only the Academy could provide.

Alamina agreed, reluctantly, not wishing to see her go but reassuring herself that Ethelinda would certainly return to reunite with her children.

Except she never did.

She had left behind the crystal ball, along with a

magical talisman called the Compass of the Seventh Kingdom, which had been in her family for as long as anyone could remember. According to Ethelinda, it could point the way toward any destination the holder held constant in her mind.

"Why not take the compass with you?" Alamina had asked her. "It could help you find your husband."

But Ethelinda seemed sure that there was some greater purpose for the compass. Her father, she said, had entrusted it to her, saying it was meant for "the one who would put directions aright and weave the strands of time together as they ought to be." Her father had known of Ethelinda's gift, and had believed she was that person. But Ethelinda had never thought it so. She believed it was meant for Alamina—or that Alamina knew who that person might be. She wasn't sure which, but she insisted that Alamina keep it safe and not part with it for any reason, until such time as its purpose became known.

Now, that time was close at hand.

Alamina opened the third drawer of the desk in her office and reached into a hidden compartment at the back, where the compass lay hidden. She removed it from the box where it had been kept since Ethelinda gave it to her: a square red-and-gold container covered with intricate designs and adorned with precious gems. A few rays of bright sunlight streamed through her office window and glinted off the compass' golden surface as she held it in her hands, running her fingers along its edges. The needle spun in circles, uncertain of which way it should direct her, just as she was uncertain about which way to go. She hoped the days ahead would provide clarity, because those days were dwindling in number. The time was nearly upon her to act—to correct the mistake she had made twenty years ago.

The three boys entered detention hall one after the other: Joey, followed by Vano, followed by Django. They went directly to three desks in the front row, which Alamina knew they had occupied on several occasions when she had monitored detention before. They were no strangers to detention hall. The only thing that seemed to surprise them on this particular day was the fact that they were the only ones there.

"What have we done now, Mama?" said Django. "None of our teachers said we were in trouble—this time."

Alamina scowled at them from behind the teacher's desk in front of the room. "You've been in enough trouble to sit in detention every day from now until you graduate," she said. "And don't call me 'Mama.'"

"Sorry, Mama," said Django.

Vano flashed a grin, which vanished when Alamina turned her gaze on him. She was, in fact, something of a surrogate mother to the three—even if she had kept this fact confidential among them—and she regretted that she hadn't been able to instill in them the same kind of discipline that most other pupils developed voluntarily. It seemed ironic that she was so well-liked by most of the Academy students, but that these three, who were most directly in her charge, were most likely to defy her.

She paused, thinking.

"On second thought," she said finally, "you *can* call me that. Or you will be able to start calling me that when we go on our field trip."

Joey threw up both hands and let out a WHOOP! It was echoed by Vano.

"Field trip! Yay!" Django shouted.

Alamina frowned at them and slapped the palm of her hand on the desk in front of her, silencing the three.

"Field trips, as you know, are exercises in learning," she said. "They are not an excuse to shirk your studies. You will be responsible for completing all your regular assignments, on time, even though you will have less time to do so. Do you understand?"

They all nodded.

"Now," she continued, "this will be something more than a typical field trip. We will be entering the labyrinth."

They all just sat there, looking at her.

"But, Mama," Vano said finally, "the labyrinth hasn't

been seen in years. We've never even seen it *at all*."

The others nodded in agreement. Alamina had to admit this *could* be a problem. She was relying on the legend that said the labyrinth appeared to a Pathfinder in times of great need. She *was* a Pathfinder, and she couldn't imagine a much greater need than the one she faced now.

"Let me worry about that," she said.

"Are we going to do a time jump?" Joey asked.

"No."

"Then, what...?"

"I've decided you should have a lesson in your heritage. You were both very young when your mother left the Black Forest," Alamina said, looking in turn at Vano and Joey. "And you," she nodded toward Django, "weren't even born yet. So, I thought it might be a good idea to take you back there for a visit."

Joey shook his head. "Why not just buy us plane tickets?"

"Because that wouldn't give you any idea of your culture," Alamina said. "Besides," she said, "I need your help with a special task."

If she had gotten their attention by mentioning the labyrinth, this new piece of information really got them to sit up and take notice.

"We're going to enter the labyrinth as a full Romani caravan," she continued. "We'll build our own wagons once we're inside. And we'll have to take a few of the other students and faculty with us, but you three will be key to the success of our task." She turned her gaze on Django. "How are you doing in your theater class?"

"All A's, Mama," he beamed.

"Good." Any other time, she would have taken him to task for the C's and D's he was getting in his other mundane courses; under the circumstances, though, his acting ability was all that mattered. Her eyes darted from Django to Vano to Joey and back again. "You will *all* have to play your roles perfectly," she admonished them. "No one can know who we really are, or why we're there."

Joey looked back at her, an unspoken question in his eyes.

Vano gave it voice: "Why?"

Alamina glared at them, letting her disapproving eyes fall on each in turn. "This is why you need to *study*, gentlemen," she said. "I *know* each of you has taken Advanced Temporal Management..."

They nodded.

"...and read the textbook of the same title."

"Kind of," Vano said.

"That's the problem," she said. Reaching into a desk drawer and producing a copy of the text in question, she stood, moved around to the front of the desk and deposited it directly in front of Vano. "The kind of task we are about to undertake requires a *thorough* and *detailed* knowledge of temporal management."

"But you said we weren't going to time jump," Django protested.

"If you'd read even the introduction to this book, you would know that the principles of temporal management apply to the present day," she said. "Our present is someone else's future, and another person's past."

In this case, she said to herself, *mine*.

"Can anyone tell me the sixth principle of temporal management?"

Vano raised his hand. "Time does not exist, except as a measurement of reality."

Alamina rolled her eyes. "No, Vano. That is the *first* principle. I can see how far you got in our textbook."

The other two laughed.

"I take it you know, then, Joey," she said, turning suddenly to him.

"The River of Time flows in two directions at once?" he tried, hopefully.

"That's true," she mused, "but it's not even covered in this text!"

This was taking far too long. If she insisted that they keep on guessing, they might be here all afternoon. "The sixth principle of time management is the principle of discretion," she said, answering her own question. She picked up the book, opened it to the third chapter, and read: "Discretion is necessary whenever one attempts to manipulate time. If you are discovered seeking to alter the course of human or natural events, you will not only fail, you will put yourself and any accomplices at risk."

Django smiled a devilish smile. "So, we are to be your accomplices, Mama?"

Alamina slammed the book shut and dropped it with a loud THWACK! on the desk in front of Django.

Then she stared in dismay as the book flickered and faded, turning briefly translucent before regaining its fully solid form. It was the same thing that had happened to the headmaster before he disappeared those many years ago, and it had happened again, every so often, since then. Mostly, it had affected little things: a pencil, a notebook, things nobody would notice unless they were looking for them. Once, a desk had gone missing, but everyone just assumed one of the custodians had misplaced it. Everyone, that is, except Alamina.

Recently, more and more items had been "misplaced," and even one of the students turned up missing. She was discovered, safe and sound, back at home with her parents. But she had no memory of ever having been at the Academy at all. When two instructors visited her parents' home and asked her why she had left campus, she called them crazy. She said she'd never even heard of the place, and her parents said she'd been going to the local public school all along.

This was getting serious. If Alamina did not act, she realized, everything about the Academy might disappear and revert to what it had been before. It would no longer be the Academy of the Lost Labyrinth; it would, once more, be merely Ridley Manor.

"Whoa!" said Django.

He and his brothers had seen it, too, but she didn't have time to explain it to them. The time was too short and the stakes were too high.

"This is not a game, gentlemen. It is not a written exam. We are going into the *labyrinth*! If we fail in our purpose, the chances are high—overwhelmingly so—that we might become lost inside it. I've been there. I nearly got lost inside myself. I do *not* want that to happen to you."

Then, under her breath to herself, she said, "I promised your mother I would care for you."

It was time, she knew, to show them the Compass of the Seventh Kingdom. She pulled it out of a pouch that had been hanging at her belt and held it in front of her for them to see. "This belonged to your mother," she said, as they leaned in for a closer look. "It will help us find the person we're looking for. He's a little boy named Alexander, and he holds the key to saving our school. And the world."

She would need the crystal ball, as well. She made a mental note to pack it for the journey ahead—and hoped the journey would be possible. She turned away from the three boys and strode over to the window, trying to appear confident. In fact, however, she was terrified. She was scared it wouldn't be there, and if it wasn't, she didn't know what she would do.

She closed her eyes as she pulled back the shades that blocked the window, then opened them, apprehensive.

She didn't realize she'd been holding her breath when she exhaled a sigh of deep relief.

There, below, she saw something she hadn't seen in twenty years.

The labyrinth was back.

Chapter Three

Corn and Ivy

The scarecrow seemed to cast a shadow against the sky. There was a full moon, but the rest of the cloudless veil was blacker than it should have been.

Halloween was almost over.

The scruffy old man in the rickety ticket booth called out, "Fifteen minutes till closing."

The boy with the tousled dark brown hair was the only one there to hear him.

His given name (the boy's, that is) was Alex, which was short for Alexander, after the great conqueror, the long-ago king of Macedonia.

The boy was there by himself at the entrance to the corn maze on the outskirts of Moravia, Iowa, the entrance to which was guarded by the silent scarecrow. It didn't seem to bother the scruffy old man in the rickety ticket booth that Alex was there by himself. An orphan who had lived with half a dozen foster families, he was only in his current home because his guardians needed the government stipend that came with him. They didn't much care about where he spent his time, as long as they got their check. So he had come here, to the maze, alone.

But he had paid to be there, using most of his allowance, and that was what mattered to the man in the ticket booth.

The corn maze had been open for a month, and it wouldn't be open past tonight. Unfortunately, the old man—who owned the place—had yet to earn back the money he'd put into it, because the weekend rain had kept too many customers away. He was on his hands and knees now, like a bloodhound with a saggy, weepy belly, hunting for spare coins that might have fallen through the booth's wooden slats onto the muddy-puddly ground underneath.

He muttered something: "Last time. No more."

Then he glanced at the boy again. He was not going to look for the child if he got lost. It was none of his concern. "Better get started," he called out. "Fourteen minutes."

The boy stared up at the nameless scarecrow, which seemed to stare back at him, though this was, of course, impossible. The paint that had been used to create its mouth ran down its chin, where the earlier rains had carried it. One of its eyes, which previously had been potatoes, had sprouted roots that clawed blindly at the night. The other had gone missing altogether, as someone had removed it.

"I did it! Rrawk!

The voice caught the boy's attention, and he looked around to see where it had come from.

Its owner was dark as the night itself. But then, the boy saw movement: a glisteny, feathery head, pecking persistently at the potato-eye that remained.

"What is your name?" the boy asked.

"Rrawk!" came the reply.

"Pleased to meet you, Mr. Roark."

"Rrawk!"

"Mr. Rrawk, then. Beg your pardon."

He wondered how the crow could speak, but he didn't think much more about it, because it clearly *had* spoken, and there was no disputing that fact. There was, therefore, no use in worrying too much about it. Besides, the night was getting on, and the air was growing chill. The boy felt his goose-bumped skin give a fateful shiver beneath his winter jacket, whereupon an idea occurred to him. It was little more than a fancy, but a real idea nonetheless.

"Mr. Rrawk, since you can fly, might you be willing

to guide me through this corn maze?"

The one who called himself Rrawk said "Rrawk!" again, as if to make sure the boy knew that was his name. Then, he said, "That would be cheating."

The shadow of a frown drifted across the boy's face against the dark night. No matter, then. It had been worth a try. Even so, the boy was lonely. He had been lonely for as long as he could remember *being* anything. And so, he opened his mouth again and ventured the admit: "I would be grateful, at the least, for your company."

The crow seemed not to hear him, intent as he was at pecking the potato eye.

Alex was not too disappointed. Rrawk was, in fact, only a crow.

The crow paused in his pecking. "Heard that!" he squawked.

Alex tilted his head to one side. "Heard what?"

"That thing you said. In your head."

"You couldn't have. I didn't say it."

"Ah, but you did. To yourself. And your self is the most important audience." He bowed like an actor on stage at the end of a performance.

The brows over Alex's young eyes pressed down on them. "Then what did I say?"

"That would be telling!"

Alex did not believe the crow had heard anything,

nor was he even sure, any longer, that he even wanted the creature's company. So, instead of pursuing the matter further, he set his eyes once again upon the corn maze and put his feet upon the path that conveyed him thence.

The crow finished his meal and followed.

So did the scarecrow.

The moon was full and the sky was dark half a world away, as well. Time was not the same on the rolling hills of Yorkshire, running behind the age where Alex dwelt by nearly a century. These were still the days of horse and carriage, though the age of the automobile was soon to dawn. Electric lights were recent inventions, airplanes were still a fantasy, and motion pictures a soon-to-be-realized dream.

A girl named Elizabeth, after the queen, stood in the garden behind Ridley Manor, with its fifty rooms.

A gas light burned in but a single one.

Ivy clambered up thick stone walls and entwined itself around the clawed feet of gargoyles who stood sentinel at the roofline.

The girl stood as still as one of them, dark eyes wide like saucers at a mad tea party, magnified all the more by a pair of spectacles that she preferred not to wear but had to on occasion. Her auburn hair flowed in rivulets over her slender shoulders. She had been reading before she'd come down to the garden, beckoned by a passage from a novel that had taken her fancy: "I only wanted to see what the garden was like, your Majesty."

And it had struck her, upon reading these words, that she had always wanted to see what the garden behind Ridley Manor was like. Though she had lived there all her days, she could not remember ever exploring it—and, oddly, even when she looked down on it from her second-floor bedroom, she realized she had never noticed the thing that seemed to be at the heart of it: a grand labyrinth. Dense and green in shrub and ivy, it had always seemed darker than it should have been. And on this, the darkest of full-moon nights, it seemed darker still.

Elizabeth turned back toward the manor and saw the lamp still burning in her window. She should return and attend to it, she told herself, but before she could take a step in that direction, a noise distracted her. It had come from the direction of the labyrinth, and before she could wonder if she had imagined it, it came again.

"Who?" it said.

"I beg your pardon," the girl replied.

"Who... are you seeking?"

A flitter-flutter of wings defied the silence, and a long-eared owl descended from a hidden nest inside the bush-maze.

"Whom," the girl rejoined. She had learned her

letters well, and memorized the rules of grammar.

"Who!" the owl repeated.

"I do not wish to argue, Miss Owl. I only came to see the labyrinth."

"Oh, but you cannot see it from there," the owl said, ignoring the debate over who or whom.

"I can, indeed," the girl protested. "I *am* wearing my spectacles!"

"Argumentative child." The owl made a noise that sounded like "Pfft," although it seemed to the girl that producing such a noise would have required lips. Elizabeth was highly intelligent, because she thought about things a lot. Sometimes, she thought about them so much that she forgot to do anything about them, and just stood there contemplating them in the mirror of her mind. She was doing this now.

"You can only truly see from within," said the owl. "So it is with the labyrinth, as it is with yourself."

"Silly owl. I knew that, of course."

A soft wind trifled with the leaves of the garden, caressing them with an unseen hand.

"Then tell me this," the owl responded, cocking her head to one side. "How did Ridley Manor get its name?"

"A riddle?"

"But of course! Exactly that!"

Elizabeth tapped her toe on the stone pathway. "And I suppose you wish me to solve it."

"What I wish is not at issue here. It is your wish that matters. What do you wish?"

The girl sighed in exaggerated fashion. "To know the answer to your riddle."

"Then you must enter it."

"The riddle?"

"Yes."

The owl cocked her head toward the labyrinth, and the girl raised an eyebrow. "If you enter the riddle, you will find what you truly wish."

The girl thought for a moment. She remembered from her studies, that the labyrinth had been constructed to keep something inside. She could not recall what that something was, but it occurred to her that the labyrinth might have seemed very much like a riddle to anyone imprisoned within it.

"How long has this labyrinth been here?" she asked, realizing at once how silly it must have sounded posing such a question to an owl.

"Does it matter?"

"Who planted it?"

"You did."

Well, that made absolutely no sense at all. She was just a young girl, and the labyrinth was made up of fully grown shrubs and hedges that were taller than she was. It had obviously been there for quite some time—even if, somehow, she had never noticed it before. She could not possibly have planted it. ... The owl was clearly playing games with her.

She set her tone in challenge. "If you are so very wise, help me find my way through the labyrinth."

"Wisdom finds its own way," said the owl.

"Oh, you are no help whatsoever!" Elizabeth exclaimed. "I don't need your guidance, owl. I can do this on my own!"

She failed to notice, in her pique, that the owl had just finished telling her as much. Or that, of a sudden, she was no longer scared of the labyrinth. When one is determined to do a thing, fear tends to be forgotten. Taking exaggerated steps to make her point, she strode resolutely toward the entrance and disappeared inside.

The owl followed.

Now, the ivy from the labyrinth was the very same ivy that wound itself around the feet of the gargoyles perched on high. And when it rustled in the night breeze, it called to them.

And they, too, followed.

Chapter Four

Fowl Play

The corn maze wound down and around and up and through, back in on itself and across again. It reminded Alex of learning to tie his shoe. He'd been stubborn about that. Instead of observing how others did it and copying them, he had insisted on figuring it out himself—and in consequence had created all manner of intricate knots that were nearly impossible to untangle.

"Rrawk! Where are you going?"

The boy turned around, surprised. "Are you still there? I thought you weren't coming."

"That's what you get for thinking."

"I suppose so," the boy said coolly. He was not about to admit that he was glad for the company, or that he was hopelessly lost. Already he had been inside the maze long enough that he imagined the proprietor had closed the rickety ticket booth and gone home.

"Lost?" asked the crow.

"No," said the boy.

"Lost," the crow declared.

The boy stopped and sat down on a hay bale, in exaggerated fashion, as though admitting defeat. He avoided looking at the crow, and instead focused his attention on pulling bits of hay from the bale, one by one.

"You won't find your way like that."

Alex raised his head and fixed the crow with a withering gaze. "*You* said you wouldn't help me."

"Rrawk! I did not!" The crow seemed wounded. "I only declined to guide you, not to help you!"

The boy was about to say something more, known only to him, but the crow did not wait for his answer and instead flew away in a scurry-flurry of night-black wings.

"Figures," Alex muttered, pulling more bits of hay from the bale as he sulked.

"Yes, it does."

The boy's head shot up at the sound of a voice that was not the crow's. It was higher-pitched and scratchy like an opera singer with straw stuffed down her throat. It belonged, as it happened, to the scarecrow.

"How did you find me?" asked the boy.

"It was not easy, let me tell you, since that evil crow plucked out my eyes!"

"He did not seem evil to me," said Alex. "Just annoying."

"You might feel differently if he'd plucked out *your* eyes," said the scarecrow.

Alex had to admit that this was true.

"Well, what do you want, then?"

"Revenge, of course!" said the scarecrow, as though it should have been self-evident. "If you help me get it, I will be your guide." She nodded her head, and it fell off. Fortunately, she caught it before it hit the ground and resituated it on the space between her shoulders. (Alex assumed it was a "she" from the sound of the scarecrow's voice, although there was honestly no other way to tell.)

Alex noticed for the first time that she was carrying something: a bow and a quiver full of arrows. He was sure he would have seen it if she'd had it outside the maze, and he had no idea where she might have gotten it. Of course, he had no idea how she managed to move at all, let alone converse with him, in the first place, so it wasn't as shocking as it might have been otherwise.

"For you," she said, handing him the bow and removing the quiver to offer it, as well.

The boy took it reluctantly, amid the nagging feeling that it wasn't exactly a gift. "What am I supposed to do with this?" he asked.

"Why shoot him, of course," said the scarecrow, as though it should have been as plain as day—even though it was night.

The boy shook his head. "I can't do that. That would be murder."

"Yes, a murder of crows!" the scarecrow threw back her head and laughed at her own joke. "Or in this case, one crow."

Alex didn't understand the joke, but he didn't care to.

The scarecrow suddenly stopped laughing, and her raspy voice turned quite serious. "You will need my help to reach the center of the maze," she warned. "And you must reach the center before you can get back out."

Alex scuffed his heel against the dirt path. That didn't make sense. "I can just go back the way I came," he said.

The scarecrow laughed again, but there was less mirth in her tone this time. "And which way would that be?"

She had a point. Alex doubted he could retrace his steps and find his way out quickly on his own. But how big could the maze be? He was bound to stumble upon the exit eventually, even if he had to go push his way through spaces in the walls. Except there were no spaces in the walls. The corn grew so thick he could not even *see* through it, let alone *walk* through it. Even if he could, would he be closer or farther from the exit? There was no way of knowing.

"I don't know," he confessed.

"Then we have a deal," the scarecrow said firmly. "We will wait here until the crow returns, you will shoot him, and I will take you to the center of the maze."

Alex frowned. "Why don't you just shoot him yourself?"

"It's against the rules."

"What rules?"

"We're only supposed to scare the crows, not kill them. It's written down in triplicate, and all of us are required to sign in blood. Please don't make me fetch you a copy."

Alex shook his head, idly wondering whose blood was used, considering scarecrows did not seem to have any.

"Then it's settled," the scarecrow said.

Alex said nothing. He just sat there, trying to figure out what he would do if and when Mr. Rrawk returned.

It seemed to Elizabeth that she had been walking for hours, though she had no way of knowing how long it had been. It was still dark out, but a bank of clouds had rolled in, obscuring moon and stars, and bringing with it a light but steady drizzle. Before long, it had woven itself into the strands of the girl's hair, matting it against her head, and chilling her skin where it pressed against her sopping-soaked rose-red dress.

Her new shoes squished-squashed, sinking into the ground as it became muddy, and she shivered involuntarily. It was time to go back, she decided. But the moment she turned around, she found her way blocked by a wall of ivy. *That* hadn't been there before. She knew it hadn't. There came from the underbrush a skittering sound, like an animal scurrying away. The leaves moved, but she saw no sign of furry feet, then realized that the plants themselves were moving, changing the shape of the path as she moved along it and blocking any possible retreat.

Elizabeth gasped. "How will I ever get back?" she asked no one in particular.

"Who?"

She looked up at the owl. "Me, that's who! You might have told me the labyrinth would change as I went forward."

The owl puffed out her chest feathers and turned her head almost all the way around, then back again. "I thought you knew," she said, almost haughtily. "Life is always like that. You never know where you might go, but 'back' is not an option."

"It can be for me!" Elizabeth said, though she didn't know exactly why.

"Perhaps," said the owl. "But not here, and not now."

Elizabeth was growing impatient. "*You* know where you're going," she said. "You can see it all from overhead! Can you tell me the best way?"

"Forward," Miss Owl hooted. "Always forward!"

The foul fowl was no help at owl.

Just then, a strand of ivy flashed upward from the midst of the labyrinth like a bolt of green lightning in reverse. Before poor Miss Owl could react, it had latched onto her and whipped itself around her left leg, then her right, and began to pull her violently down toward the ground. The girl watched in horror as she thrashed about, and took a step backward as a winged stone gargoyle emerged from the green wall just behind her and began advancing on its trophy.

Elizabeth wanted to run, but the way backward was blocked, and the gargoyle had placed itself between her and the path ahead. She was amazed to hear Miss Owl shriek, not in panic, but in counsel: "Fear not the obstacle before you! Fear only the one inside you!"

In the owl's selfless wisdom, Elizabeth somehow found her courage. With a cry, she rushed toward the gargoyle and, closing her eyes tightly, threw herself at it with all the strength she could muster. It seemed like forever between the time her feet left the wet earth and the time she reached her quarry. And in that time, she wondered why she would do this. Why would she do such a thing on behalf of a haughty old bird, and one who had refused to help her when she'd asked? She did not have time to answer this question. She opened her eyes again and saw the stone gargoyle before her, mouth open in a hideous snarl that would have scared the wits out of the bravest soul in Yorkshire.

But she did not have time to be scared, either.

"You never have time," she thought she heard the owl say softly in a somehow distant voice. "You always think you do."

In that moment, she was upon the gruesome creature. But when she touched it, it turned to dust, crumbling all around her in a thousand million bits and pieces.

Thrown entirely off balance by this turn of events, Elizabeth tumbled like a cartwheel off its axle, legs flying and arms flailing as she fell and skidded on the muddy earth. Dizzy and befuddled, she shook her head vigorously and rose to her feet, trying in vain to wipe the mud from her rose-red dress and only smearing it all the more deeply into thread and fiber.

"Miss Owl?" she said, looking about her.

But the wise old bird was nowhere to be seen. The strands of ivy that had held her fast lay strewn about, lifeless, on the earth; yet she herself was gone.

There was, however, something else...

The clouds above had parted just enough to admit a sliver of pale moonlight, and this narrow beacon settled on the ground just before her, glinting off something half hidden in the mud.

The girl stepped forward, bent down and picked it up.

She wiped the mud off and opened it. It was a pocketwatch that looked to have been fashioned from an oyster shell that formed a perfect circle. The mechanism itself was inside the shell and seemed to have been set in a giant pearl, its gears working in perfect time as it ticked and tocked in cadence against the silent night. She opened it and saw the time was midnight now, exactly, and at the center of the watch face were two round, yellow eyes blinking back at her from another face.

"Miss Owl!"

"Now," she said, "you have time. Use it wisely."

The eyes closed and vanished in a heartbeat.

The scarecrow hid behind a corn stalk as the crow flew into view. He was carrying something in his beak and wearing something on his head, but the boy couldn't tell what either was.

"There he is! There he is!" the scarecrow whispered excitedly. "Be ready with your bow."

Alex raised the bow tentatively and aimed it in Mr. Rrawk's general direction.

"Wait till he's in range! But don't let him see you!" The tone in the scarecrow's raspy voice was a cross between giddy and desperate.

"You promise to get me out of here?" the boy asked, seeking to reassure himself and assuage his already-guilty conscience. The crow was flying nearer now, and was close to being in range. Nervously, Alex fingered the bowstring, feeling the tension, a match for the tension within him. He reminded himself of how sorry he felt for the scarecrow, at having her eyes pecked out so cruelly. But then he thought of how mean it was, also, to scare the poor bird away from his meal. He had only been hungry, after all. And if the scarecrow had let him feast on the corn, he would never have been tempted to peck out her potato-eyes! Still, he hadn't needed to do it.

"Why does life have to be so complicated?" Alex said inside his head.

The truth was, he realized, that *he* was being tempted now. Of all the reasons and motives that tumbled around inside his skull for doing the scarecrow's bidding, the one that made him even consider such a thing was his own desire. Truly. He wanted to be free of the maze. The longer he remained inside it, the more he lamented that he might never find his way out again, and it was this fear that drove him to contemplate the madness of actually shooting Mr. Rrawk.

Suddenly horrified at himself, he loosed his hold on the bowstring and watched as the arrow fell harmlessly to the earth.

An odd sound reached his ears a moment later, like two straw brooms being slapped repeatedly together.

He turned to see the scarecrow.

She was... applauding.

"Bravo! Well done!" she announced in her creaky-croaky voice as the crow descended to alight on her shoulder.

Alex's eyes went wide.

"But...," he protested.

"Rrawk!" said the crow. It sounded oddly like a laugh. "Fooled you, did we not?" he said, seeming overly pleased with himself.

"You passed our little test," the scarecrow added. "I must confess I was worried for a moment there, but you came through with flying colors."

"Test?" said Alex. "Then you are...?"

"The best of friends," the scarecrow announced. "But we had to make you think otherwise, to be sure you were worthy to reach the heart of the maze."

"We've become quite good at acting," Mr. Rrawk boasted. "She pretends she wants to scare me, so I can eat the farmer's corn."

"And he only eats the ears of corn that fall to earth, so I can keep my job!"

"But—your eyes!" exclaimed Alex.

The scarecrow chuckled. "Really, now, dear boy.

Could *you* see with a potato?"

"Well, I suppose..."

"I don't need eyes to see, in any case—no more than I need a tongue to speak."

Alex looked again at what was left of the scarecrow's painted-on mouth: the bits that hadn't run down her straw chin in the rain. "Please don't stare," she said curtly. "It's impolite. I *know* I need to do my makeup!"

The boy averted his eyes quickly. He had no wish to be rude. Or cruel, for that matter. He had been the one and nearly the other in the space of just a few minutes. Turning toward the crow, he noticed now what he was wearing on his head: It was a miniature baseball cap, embroidered with a face of a smiling bird.

"That's an oriole, not a crow," Alex observed. He certainly knew the difference, although he preferred the New York Yankees to the Baltimore Orioles. Regardless, he was quite the baseball fan, although he had never seen a game in person.

He received a small allowance from his guardians, and he typically spent it all on packs of baseball cards: Topps, Bowman, Donruss, and the glossy Upper Decks. Once they were in hand, he made sure to memorize all the important stats by all the best players, past and present, which were printed on the back. He had so many baseball cards in his collection that he had full sets from several seasons, along with duplicates of many players (usually not the prized All-Stars and Hall of Famers, but lesser ones with funny names like Razor Shines, Oil Can Boyd, and Van Lingle Mungo—an oddball asset he had found in a previous foster home's attic).

"I *realize* it's an oriole," the bird quipped. "Do you know of a team named the Crows?"

"Well, no..."

"Then I suppose a Baltimore oriole will have to do, won't it? Did you know the greatest player ever to play the game was born in Baltimore?"

Alex nodded. "Babe Ruth," he said. "But he wasn't the greatest. He wasn't even the best on his own team!"

"I thought you might say that," Mr. Rrawk continued, "which is why I brought you this."

He flew from the scarecrow's shoulder to the boy's, which took Alex by such surprise that he winced and ducked before realizing that the crow had no intention of attacking him. The bird then hopped down his arm on one foot—for he was carrying something in the other—careful not to break the boy's skin with his talons. (It rather tickled, Alex thought.) The boy reflexively opened his hand, wherein the bird deposited a small piece of cardboard encased in a clear plastic sleeve.

Alex turned it over and looked at it. He jumped in such surprise and joy that his feet actually left the ground.

"A Lou Gehrig baseball card!" he exclaimed.

"If I'm not mistaken, it's older than any of those you have in your collection," the scarecrow observed.

"And more valuable, too," Mr. Rrawk chimed in.

"Yes!" Alex said, giddy. Indeed, Alex didn't have any cards nearly as old as the 1925 black-and-white card, emblazoned with Gehrig's full name, Henry L. Gehrig, in the lower left-hand corner. Most of his cards were far more recent, purchased in bubblegum packs displayed at the drugstore checkout stand.

Lou Gehrig had always been his favorite.

"How did you know?" he said.

"It's easier to know things in the maze," the scarecrow answered, as though this were self-evident.

Alex had always wanted to own cards showing players like Babe Ruth and Ty Cobb and Dizzy Dean: players who had made the game great. But he had wanted a Gehrig card more than any other, because he knew the story of the man they called the Iron Horse.

Gehrig had earned that nickname because he'd appeared in more games without missing a single one than any other player in the history of baseball: two-thousand, one-hundred and thirty. Alex had memorized that statistic, and it had always amazed him that a man could have played in every single game for the New York Yankees over the course of fourteen years. Babe Ruth hit more home runs, but he could never match that!

As Alex reflected on these things, he heard voices inside his head. Where they came from, he couldn't be sure.

If they say it cannot be done,
you can be the only one!
Time stands still
for the one who stands firm.
The one who perseveres
will get from there to here.

Alex suddenly remembered his manners. "Thank you so much!" he said.

"Thank yourself," said the scarecrow, and the boy watched in amazement as she vanished before his eyes.

"Where did she...?" he started to ask the crow. But Mr. Rrawk was nowhere to be seen.

"He must have flown off," the boy muttered to himself, unwilling to admit that he would have seen a fluttering of feathers from the corner of his eye and felt the crow—who had, after all, been perched upon his shoulder—lift off and take to flight. It could not possibly have been all in his head, now, could it? No. He glanced down and saw that he still held the Lou Gehrig card in his hand.

It looked, he thought, a tad peculiar, though. It was something in the eyes. They didn't look quite human, and they appeared to be all black. As he stared at them for several moments, Alex would have sworn that one of them winked at him.

"Mr. Rrawk?" he breathed.

It winked again.

Chapter Five

Waylaid

The clouds again obscured the stars, and a chill breeze blew through the labyrinth, dipping down into its winding corridor so that the girl was not spared its ire. Elizabeth did not know whether to be grateful that the rain that soaked her had ceased, or to be disconsolate about the snow that now replaced it. It hurried and scurried in flurries on the north wind, chasing her along as though it were a border collie nipping at the heels of a wayward lamb.

Snowflakes began to stack up, one atop the other and all atop the green wall of foliage that kept Elizabeth hemmed in. They fell on the path before her, too, some of them melting partway to create a slushy, muddy mess that looked a bit—but she was quite sure didn't taste—like chocolate ice cream.

The snow shouldn't have surprised her. It was, after all, just before Christmas. Elizabeth had all but forgotten that, however, since—for reasons of her own—she tended to put that particular holiday out of her mind.

"Oh, bother," she said, barely catching herself as she nearly slipped and fell on the icy path. At least the labyrinth had stopped changing shape around her, but she still had no way back because it had already grown there, and it was impossible to tell whether the way forward was clear or blocked. Or impossibly convoluted. She felt like she had been walking half the night and should have been clear of the place by now, but she hadn't even reached the center, as far as she could tell.

The snow seemed to fall more heavily, the farther the girl progressed, and through the snowy screen, she saw a large shadowy figure appear up ahead. Somehow, it stood out against the darkness: A silver glow seemed to emanate from it.

Elizabeth stopped where she stood and raised a hand to shield her eyes, not wanting to get any closer without knowing what stood in front of her. It was certainly large, and not in the shape of a person. It was, clearly, an animal of some sort, a fact that made her all the more reticent to approach it. Animals were unpredictable, even the tame ones. She'd been thrown from a horse when she was learning to ride: It had reared at the sound of a hunter's gunshot. Another time, she had gone to visit a family friend near Pocklington, and a friendly German shepherd had bounded out from behind a hedge and leapt at her. The animal had only wanted to greet her, but she'd been very small at the time and, in its excitement, it had knocked her to the ground. She still had nightmares about it, in which the dog was reimagined as a giant snarling wolf.

Whatever stood ahead of her in the labyrinth didn't *look* like a wolf, or even a dog. It was, in fact, much larger and appeared, through the snowfall, as though it wore a crown upon its head. She felt like its eyes were upon her, studying her. Did it think of the girl as prey? Was it getting ready to charge? What *was* it? With the snow falling heavily from the gray-black sky, she still could not be sure. Her curiosity was beginning to make war against her fear, demanding that she know. Besides, she reasoned, there was no way to go but forward, and the animal was blocking her path. She had no other choice, not really.

Elizabeth took a tentative step toward it and heard her foot squish-scrunch on the half-muddy, half-frozen path.

The animal did not move.

She put a hand out against the hedge, as much to steady her convictions as her balance, and took another step.

The animal seemed frozen in place, more frozen even than the snow and ice.

A third step. She might have been able to see more clearly, but the snow seemed to fall more thickly each time she moved forward. It was so dark, in any event, that she could only see that silver glow surrounding it, and much of that reflected off the soft white, whispered snow.

Still, the animal didn't move.

She crept slowly nearer, squinting her eyes as the snow fell still more heavily, until she was nearly upon it. She could hear it breathing; see the chest expanding and contracting. It stood as tall as she was, and the "crown," she now realized, was a magnificent set of antlers. They were almost as long as the animal was tall, and she had never seen anything like it. It was like a deer, only larger, more majestic. She was certain it was not native to Yorkshire, and that it must have been brought here by someone from very far away. Who would do such a thing, and why? She had no way of knowing.

Puffs of steam escaped the animal's nostrils, wafting out into the chill night air. At last, the snow seemed to abate just a little, and she could see more clearly as the animal dipped its head toward her, dark eyes blinking lazily as it stared at her.

It? It must be a "him," with antlers as large as these.

She stretched one hand forward, tentatively, and touched the great beast's forehead, whereupon he nodded slightly in assent.

"Do you speak as well, like Miss Owl?" she asked.

He did not answer, and she assumed he was either shy or, more probably, an ordinary animal that lacked the capacity to speak. As she was thinking this, the animal pulled back from her, tossed back his head, and emitted a sound that was a little like a grunt and a little like a bark.

The girl jumped back in surprise at the sudden movement, but it was clear the animal had no wish to alarm her. Elizabeth steadied herself and waited, and the animal repeated the motion, grunting, it seemed, somewhat more urgently this time.

Elizabeth waited, and so did the animal, but when she did nothing, the creature made the same motion a third time, the grunt more like a honking now. Each time, he tossed his head in the same direction: behind and beyond him, where the path led onward. She realized he wanted her to follow.

"All right, then," she said, and nodded her own head in the same direction.

The animal must have understood her, because he grunted softly and turned around; then, to her amazement, he knelt down right there in the pathway, and a voice inside her head said, "*Climb aboard!*" It was not her own voice, nor was it anything her ears could detect. She realized it must have come from the animal, whatever *kind* of animal it was.

"*Caribou*," came the response. It could read her thoughts, as well!

"I've never heard of that," she said aloud as she climbed on.

"Ouch! Don't pull the fur, please! And no need to speak aloud. I know your thoughts the moment you think them."

"Sorry," Elizabeth said.

"*Sorry*," she repeated in her thoughts. She found it mildly disconcerting that the... Care-i-boo... which she had never heard of, knew what she was thinking. She was used to letting her thoughts out at her own discretion, not having them taken from her before she was ready to share them. "*What is a Care-i-boo*?" she asked, enunciating each of the syllables in exaggerated fashion as she settled onto the creature's back. A moment later, he rose to his feet as he stood, jostling her so much that she nearly fell off. She started to panic, recalling the time she had been thrown from the horse, and grabbed on to the caribou's fur again.

"*Ouch!*" he said again, accompanied by an audible grunt of surprise and dismay. "*Please! If you need to steady yourself, use the antlers.*"

"*Right.*" Elizabeth hastily let go of the caribou's fur and placed both hands on his antlers.

"*Much better, thank you.*" The caribou said as he began to amble forward. Elizabeth got the feeling that he was moving quickly, for him, even though his pace was rather plodding. She sensed, too, in his thoughts, a certain urgency. Something was amiss that had him concerned. And, for some reason, her presence was required.

"*A caribou,*" he said, addressing her earlier query, "*is what you might know as a reindeer.*"

Elizabeth vaguely remembered hearing of reindeer, but she could not place where she had heard of them. Had she cared more about Christmas, she might have known, for then she would have read the poem entitled *A Visit from St. Nicholas,* wherein they were first mentioned. In fact, her mother had once read to her this very poem, but she had dismissed it from her mind, as she had all else to do with the holiday. As has been mentioned, she did this for reasons of her own.

"*If you are a reindeer,*" she asked, "*does that mean you like the rain?*"

The caribou chuckled. "*Reins, as in reins on a horse,*" he answered. "*They aren't very comfortable, but they are necessary to perform the task I'm charged with.*" Elizabeth sensed a hint of pride in the caribou's thought-voice at this last statement. He seemed to consider this task, whatever it was, quite important.

"*Oh,*" she thought. "*Do you have a name?*"

"*Most people call me Comet, because I'm so fast,*" he

declared. "*But you may call me Cary.*"

As Cary loped along, it seemed to Elizabeth he didn't seem fast at all. Cary seemed a much better name, especially since he was carrying her.

"*Don't get used to that,*" he quipped. "*I am NOT a beast of burden!*"

His ability to read her thoughts would take some getting used to.

"*You should be grateful you can do it,*" he said. "*Only those capable of believing the greatest things can hear thought voices. It's a pity you don't believe in Christmas, but I have a feeling that will change. Ha!*"

Elizabeth didn't know what he meant by that, but she had a feeling she was about to find out.

The shadow was darker than the night itself. It hovered over the boy, but it did not belong to him. Where it came from was impossible to see, but Alex knew one thing about it: It was in front of him, whichever way he turned, and it made finding his way out of the corn maze that much more difficult.

The darkness seemed to breathe and seethe, like an angry blacksmith's bellows stoking a hot, invisible flame. It rustled through the corn stalks like a palpable wind, taking form gradually as a thousand coal-black wings that took to the air and rushed at Alex as if from nowhere.

The boy ducked, then fell to his knees beneath the bat wings that buffeted the night, fighting against it even as they became one with it. He screamed as they flew at him, parting just in time to rush on a wind of their own making past his ears and over his head.

Then, they were gone, and the night was still once more.

But the shadow remained.

And out of it, straight in front of Alex as he rose to his feet, strode a short figure in peasant's garb no taller than himself. Slightly hunched over and barefoot, he clenched a large smoking pipe between his teeth, from which there rose a dancing flame. He wore a peaked, flat checkerboard cap, and a wiry tuft of beard sprouted from his angular chin.

"Who are you?" said Alex, who was less scared of this newcomer than he had been of the bats. For one thing, the diminutive pipe-smoker was no taller than he was. For another, he seemed to be a bit scared himself, or, at the very least, perturbed. Beady eyes darted this way and that, and he kept looking over his shoulder to see if someone or something was behind him. He chewed on his pipe almost voraciously, and the flame that rose from the end of it flounced and bounced about as he did. The boy could tell the little man couldn't be trusted, but he sensed more mischief than meanness in him.

It took a moment for the boy's question to register with the distracted man, but when it did, he blinked twice and faced Alex full-on. "Oh. Sorry," he said, taking the pipe from his mouth. "King Goldemar, at my service," he said, bowing stiffly.

"Don't you mean, 'at your service?'" Alex said.

"No, I don't," the man said. "Kings only serve themselves."

"Kings are supposed to wear crowns and fancy clothes," said Alex. "The way I see it, you don't look much like a king."

The little man straightened his hunched back as much as Alex guessed he could, and tugged downward on the ends of a too-short lime green vest. "Most people can't see me at all, so consider yourself blessed, young man," he said. Then he boasted: "And I *am* a king. I'm the king of the kobolds. Not that I care if you believe me." He snorted.

"I don't know what a kobold is," Alex told him.

"Well, now you do," Goldemar said, sweeping both arms outward in a flourish before him. It seemed more mocking than sincere.

"All right," said Alex. "What do you want with me?"

"You have been summoned," Goldemar said, and the moment he did so, his eyes began darting back and forth again.

That seemed, to the boy, unlikely. No one knew he

was here except for the owner of the maze, who had shown no interest in him before and would have returned home long before this. His eyes narrowed. "I don't believe you," he said matter-of-factly. "Who would have summoned me? No one knows or cares that I'm here."

"*He* knows," Goldemar said. "He knows everything."

That seemed most improbable. "Who is *he*?" Alex said, mimicking Goldemar's tone.

"My master."

"But you said you were a king!"

"I am a king," the little man protested. "Stop asking so many questions. Just follow me. He isn't particularly patient." Goldemar was getting more agitated.

Alex didn't answer right away. He wanted a moment to think, and besides, he rather enjoyed making the impatient imp wait.

Finally, he said: "If I go with you, will you show me the way out of this maze?"

The kobold was tapping his toe impatiently on the ground. "Yes, yes. Of course I will. It's very easy. But you must go to the center of the maze first, and you cannot get there unless you follow me."

Alex wasn't sure whether to believe Goldemar. In fact, he was pretty sure he *didn't* believe him. Moreover, he didn't like the way this 'master' of his made the kobold act, and he was not eager to meet him. Not at all. Still, he had no better option, when it came right down to it. He was no closer to—and, for all he knew, was farther away from—finding a way out than he had been before. He didn't trust this "king" Goldemar at all, but he trusted his own ability to find his way out, being upside-down and turned around as he was.

"All right," he said finally. "I'll come with you, but if you don't keep your promise to me, I'll..." He didn't say anything more. The boy remembered he had been taught not to threaten people, and even though this kobold was not a human person, he suspected that lesson applied to him, too—even if Goldemar *was* the most annoying individual he had come across in quite some time.

The kobold turned and started ambling, almost running, back the way he had come, into the darkness.

Alex stood there, watching him, still unsure whether he should follow or just let the little man go on his way. But a few steps on, when the blackness had almost enveloped him, the kobold stopped and glanced back over his shoulder, beckoning: "Hurry!" he called back. "We mustn't keep him waiting!"

Despite his misgivings, the boy started after him.

Chapter Six

Wild Card

As he moved forward, the night got so dark that the boy could no longer see at all. The kobold reached back toward him with a gnarled hand, and he reluctantly took it, wincing at the feel of Goldemar's calloused fingers on his skin. It was either endure that touch or become stranded in the darkness, which he had no wish to do.

"How far is this place?" he asked.

"You will see. You will see," came the cryptic answer. The kobold seemed slightly out of breath as he hurried forward, being less fit than his young companion.

After a time, the darkness began to give way to a silvery glow, and Alex could see again. And what he saw amazed him, for he was no longer surrounded by corn stalks, but by a tall, dense thicket of trees that lined the path on either side. Alex could not see the source of the light, but it seemed to come from all around him. It was bright enough to see by, but just barely, and it made the bare trees of mid-autumn seem like wooden skeletons of some gigantic ghost.

A mist had rolled in from the depth of night, like a veil suspended over the land of the living.

"Well, it *is* Halloween," he said to himself, and remembered one of his foster parents once telling him that this was the time of year when—how had she put it?—"the veil was thinning." When time wound in and around itself, meeting at either end, that's how she had explained it, making a circle with her fingers as she explained it. And through that circle, she said, passed the souls of loved ones past and future, spirits known from memory and from hope.

The path gradually widened into a roadway, which made Alex wonder if he'd found his way out of the maze. Somehow, he didn't think so.

The kobold shuffled-scampered even faster now in front of him, panting like a hound dog running back to his master with a trophy from the hunt.

"I suppose I'm the trophy," the boy said to himself, and he didn't like the sound of that. It didn't help that that Goldemar seemed to be gripping his hand more tightly now. His fingers were being squished together mercilessly.

"Hey, that hurts!" he protested.

The kobold ignored him, which made him feel even more like captured quarry. He wondered if an iron cage awaited him at the end of the road. No matter how badly he wanted to find his way back home, this wasn't worth it. "Let me go!" he demanded, but the kobold only squeezed his hand that much tighter, and he was stronger than he looked... or perhaps just desperate. Yes, probably that.

Unable to extricate himself from Goldemar's grasp, Alex resigned himself to his predicament, running apace with the kobold to avoid being dragged along. At least, he had reason to believe, the journey was finally nearing its end. Up ahead, through the layer of mist, he could see an odd-shaped structure, rising like a giant tombstone out of the earth. At least, that's how it was shaped, but as he got closer, Alex could see it was a dwelling of some sort: tall and oddly, almost impossibly narrow. It was six stories tall, but each was only wide enough to accommodate a single, narrow room. It almost seemed as though it might fall over at any moment, like the Leaning Tower of Pisa.

"Come! He's waiting!" the kobold said.

"I know. I know," Alex said as he followed Goldemar up the steps to the tower, which seemed to have been built on a low mound. He wondered for a moment whether he could see over the corn maze and find a way back to where he'd been. Then he realized, though, that he no longer seemed to be *in* the maze at all, and that he had never seen this tower from his house or anywhere nearby. And that didn't make sense. No, not at all. In the maze, he was sure that he'd been going in circles, not really getting any farther from anywhere else, so he *should* have been able to see it. But nothing was as it should be here.

Goldemar led him up a rickety wooden staircase, where half the steps seemed to have been cracked in two from being stepped on in the middle by a giant ogre. On the other hand, they might have just been old and rotted through. It was probably that, he told himself as he tried to make sure he didn't trip on one of the broken steps. This was more difficult than it seemed, because the kobold was still pulling him along very fast and obviously was so familiar with the stairs that he knew which places to step and which ones to avoid.

Fortunately, he managed to avoid twisting an ankle or stumbling face-first forward, following the kobold through a pair of oak-panel doors that had been left slightly ajar and into a dank, narrow foyer with a low ceiling that made Alex feel as though he'd stepped into an oversized coffin. The place smelled so musty he almost expected to walk through an unseen spiderweb, but he found no arachnids lurking in the shadows. In fact, nothing at all seemed *alive* here except for himself and the kobold.

A dark wind suddenly rose up from out of nowhere.

Alex saw no open window through which it might have gained access; indeed, he saw no windows in the place at all, and the door seemed to have closed of its own accord behind him. In fact, there didn't seem to be any other entrances or exits, either. There was not even any staircase that offered access to the upper floors—the ones he had seen from outside—at least, not as far as he could tell.

But the wind, as it turned out, wasn't a wind, after all. Not exactly, anyway. As Alex watched in astonishment, it began to swivel and swerve around itself, like a miniature tornado twisting itself up like a pretzel or a shoelace. Flecks of what looked like soot and ash danced around between its invisible, windswept seams, spewed out like darkened sparks and flying into the twister's orbit like tiny moons. Alex noticed something strange about them: What little light there was, they didn't seem to reflect it. The only way to distinguish them from the dreary backdrop was their relative darkness, and their movement.

The whirling ashes rushed around in a mania, circling the center of the tiny tornado. They didn't stay in that orbit long, though, falling back in upon themselves as more and more of them appeared, then coalescing into something more than ashes. More than wind. More unusual than anything the boy had ever seen. The thing that took shape was nebulous at first, and even as it began to appear more substantial, it retained a certain hazy character around the edges. It flickered like static on an old black-and-white TV screen, but silently, in shadow.

Alex rubbed his eyes with both hands, struggling to focus. But his eyes had not betrayed him, and there was no way to clear his vision. Even where the image gained substance, it seemed to flow like thick mud, but smooth and black. The boy had seen oil bubbling up out of the earth once, and it seemed closer to that than anything else, but in the form of a flowing robe so long that it covered the feet of the person—or thing—that wore it and rose up over his head in a hood that obscured all but his eyes.

Those eyes were milky white, with no pupils, which left Alex with the impression that they were staring directly through him. Or perhaps into him.

The boy shivered, and not at the cold, dank air surrounding him, and he shivered again when he saw a long object form in the figure's right hand. The heavy wooden handle rose from the ground all the way above the hooded head, terminating in a curved, silver blade that appeared sharper than any Alex had ever seen. He had, however, seen pictures of the figure that stood before him, and he knew what grown-ups had named in him stories told to him past bedtime: the Grim Reaper.

It occurred to him, in that moment, that he was about to die. Here in the middle of an endless night. Here at the edge of nowhere. Here in a building that felt for all the world, from the inside of it, like a casket made to be his final resting place.

He wanted to run, but his legs were rooted to the floor. Even had they obeyed his impulse, the kobold still had firm hold of his hand. And he was not about to let go.

Panic rose in the boy's breast, and the shivering he had experienced became shuddering, even shaking.

"But I... don't *want* to die!"

A sound like air escaping from a balloon came out of somewhere: He couldn't be sure if it was the Reaper's mouth or just in a general sense, from all over. It echoed and reverberated around the room, a ghost wind touching each of the corners in turn before it reached his ears and he realized it was a voice. It was *saying* something.

"Nooo one doesssss." The last "s" started off like a snake hissing and ended in a sound like the buzz of flies.

The boy felt this was anything but reassuring. Therefore, he did not stop shaking.

The voice came again. "Deattthhh isssss only a portal ... unlesssss you resisssst it."

This didn't make Alex feel any better, either. It was at the core of human nature to resist it, so the information seemed useless at the very best.

"You... cannot cheat time."

Alex felt desperate. He looked at the scythe the Reaper held, gleaming and shimmering like a crystal even in the dull, almost stifling murk. Then, suddenly, with his free hand—the one Goldemar wasn't holding—he reached into his pocket and produced the Lou Gehrig baseball card Mr. Rrawk had given him.

"He did!" Alex proclaimed triumphantly.

And in that moment, all his fear fled from him. Holding the card up boldly, he waved it like a flag in front of his face for the Reaper to see.

"A talisman!" the kobold exclaimed.

"Yessss. I ssseee," said the Reaper, his tone barely changing but now laced with just a hint of agitation. "Seisszzze it!"

The kobold's pipe fell out of his mouth and clattered to the floor as he grabbed at the card, but Alex was able to pull it away in the nick of time, holding it up just out of Goldemar's reach. The kobold was as short as a child, and hunched at the shoulders, as kobolds are wont to be, and his arms were stocky and stubby. As he lunged for it, though, he let loose of Alex's hand, and the boy dashed to the far side of the room. Goldemar tried to go after him, but Alex's youth made him quicker and more agile than the kobold.

The hissing sound of air escaping grew louder. "That card isssszz the only thing... protecting him!" the Reaper said, his voice louder and more insistent. "If he finds the other talisssmenssszz...!"

Alex stopped abruptly, stuck out his foot and watched Goldemar stumble over it, crashing face-first into the wooden floor. His hard head thumped against the gray stone wall, and he didn't get up. The boy thought for a moment he might be dead, but then saw his chest was still rising and falling at regular intervals. He didn't know whether to be relieved or concerned. On the one hand, the kobold had led him into a trap that had put him in mortal danger, a state he still found himself in at this moment. On the other, he didn't wish anyone ill, and Goldemar *had* promised to show him the way out of here—wherever "here" was. Not that he believed the kobold.

For good or for ill, he was on his own again, and still facing the Reaper.

"Give it toooo him!" the tall, robed figure demanded.

"To him?" the boy said, confused, looking down at Goldemar.

"Yessszz. I will not allow you to leave... until you do."

Alex thought for a moment, wondering why the Reaper would demand that he give the card to an unconscious kobold. Why wouldn't he just demand it himself, or try to take it? Unless, for some reason, he *couldn't*.

The boy hesitated, then took a step toward the Reaper. He had the germ of an idea, but he had no way of knowing whether his hunch was correct; if he was wrong, he knew the price to pay would be high, but if he was right...

The Reaper did not move forward to meet him. If

anything, he leaned back slightly.

The boy took another step, and then another. And the Reaper, grudgingly, took a step of his own.

Backward.

He was right! The Reaper was afraid of him. Or, more precisely, he was afraid of the card. That's why he had demanded that Alex give it to the unconscious kobold—he stole a glance over his shoulder to be sure Goldemar was still unconscious (he was). For some reason, the Reaper was scared of the baseball card!

Alex felt courage building within him. "What happens if I find the other talismans?" he asked.

The Reaper said nothing and retreated another step.

"You don't like this, do you?"

Again, the Reaper did not answer, but the hazy, staticky aura that surrounded him seemed to flicker and flutter more quickly. He was nervous. What could possibly scare Death itself?

Alex remembered what the Reaper had said. "You can't cheat time."

But what if he could? Anything that might cheat time would be a threat to Death, and to its purveyor.

Alex took a more resolute step forward, and the Reaper took another step back—only to find himself trapped in a corner of the room. "Tell me what happens if I find the other talismans?"

"You will... essscape."

He didn't know whether the Reaper meant he

would escape this place or whether he would escape Death. He would be happy with either result.

"How? How do I use these talismans?"

"You will know," the Reaper said. "In your moment of need, thisss will be revealed."

Alex frowned. It sounded like a trick.

He stepped right up to within a foot or two of the dark, robed figure, which towered over him, its hooded head touching the ceiling. "What other talismans are there?" the boy demanded. "Where can I find them?"

The Reaper seemed to swallow hard. "You have the Wild Card," he began. "You mussst alssso obtain the Compassss of the Sssseventh Kingdom... the Map of Gildersssleeve... the Spectacles of Samwell Spink... the Pearly Pocketwatch... the Flute of Pan's Third Daughter... and the Pathfinder of Destiny." The staticky shadow at the fringes of the darkened figure were fluctuating wildly now.

"Take me to them," Alex said firmly.

"I cannot," the Reaper protested. "I cannot leave this placssse unlessszz I am called forth to claim a life from the realm of the living. Unlessszz it is that one's fated time to die."

Alex realized this must have been why the Reaper had summoned him here: If he had been fated to die, the Reaper would have gone forth to retrieve him. Since he had not left this dingy almost-crypt, which seemed to be his dwelling place, the boy could only conclude that it had never been his fated time. The Reaper had been seeking to bend the rules by bringing him here.

"Then *tell* me where they are," Alex demanded, reaching up and shaking the card in his face.

"Sssome of them are not even… in this world," the Reaper said. "You will have to cross over into another placssse to find them."

"How can I do that?"

The boy was growing even bolder and more impatient, while the Reaper took upon himself the aspect of a coward, timid and uneasy. Though the dark figure still towered above him, Alex felt as though he were looking down on a once-dreaded figure reduced to a shadow of what he appeared to be. He held up the card directly before his Reaper's eyes—and watched in astonishment as the robed and hooded figure dissolved into nothing before him.

The boy blinked once and then again. Had he cheated Death? Or had he simply stopped Death from cheating him? Either way, he was still alive… though his situation was no better than it had been before. He considered, for a moment, trying to rouse the kobold in the hope that Goldemar might show him the way out, but he doubted the "king" would be inclined to do so after being tripped and knocked unconscious. He also doubted, furthermore, whether the kobold even *knew* the way out. He hadn't exactly seen kobolds running amok out on Highway 5. He hadn't even *heard* of kobolds when it came right down to it.

So, he stepped past the still-prone body of King Goldemar and back out the door into the cold, gray darkness, which was every bit as cold and gray and dark as it had been before.

He stepped carefully down the stairs outside the tall, old building, careful to avoid the broken ones, and looked back over his shoulder to make sure the Reaper hadn't rematerialized in order to follow him. Seeing that he hadn't, Alex concluded that he himself was still not fated to die. At least not in this place. And not at this moment.

He fingered the card in its plastic sleeve inside his pocket and thanked his lucky stars for Lou Gehrig.

Then he went on his way, moving in the direction that seemed most sensible, down behind the building, where the space between the trees narrowed once more, and a dark mist settled in just above the top of his head once again.

In a moment, he could see almost nothing, and he was forced to move forward slowly, zombie-like, with his arms stretched out in front of him to avoid bumping into some unseen obstacle. He was walking so slowly, he knew he'd never get anywhere like this, even if he was, by some happy circumstance, headed in the right direction.

What was on the other side of this mist, the boy could only guess. He only hoped it wasn't a dead end that would force him to retrace his steps and send him back the way he'd come.

Chapter Seven

Reindeer Ride

Elizabeth's bottom was getting sore. Riding on a reindeer without a saddle was not the most comfortable mode of transportation.

It didn't make her feel any better that it was getting colder, too. She couldn't remember it ever being this cold in Yorkshire, and she shivered and shook in her light dress, teeth chattering as she pulled her arms in close to her—as close as she could while keeping hold of the caribou's antlers.

"I know you're cold." Cary's thoughts invaded her mind. *"It can't be helped this far north. Think of it this way: At least you're not carrying someone on your back."*

He could certainly seem out-of-sorts at times... but

what did he mean by "this far north"? The caribou was not the speediest of creatures, by any standard, and they couldn't have come very far in the time they'd been trudging along. Elizabeth was as certain as she could be that Yorkshire never got this cold.

"We're not in Yorkshire," Cary said.

Not in Yorkshire? This was not possible. There was no way, in the wildest of wild imaginations, that they could have gone as far as Durham.

"We're not in Durham," Cary declared.

Northumberland?

"Keep going. You're getting warmer, but only a little bit."

We're actually getting colder, Elizabeth thought, and if he says we're as far north as Scotland, I'll say he's daft.

The caribou grunted, and the girl took it for a laugh.

"What's so funny?"

"You are. Have you ever heard of the Arctic Circle?"

"Of course, I have, you dullard." It wasn't a very nice name to call him, but she didn't appreciate being laughed at.

"We're inside it," he said.

Now it was Elizabeth's turn to laugh. "We couldn't be."

"Oh, but we are. I'd like you to meet someone."

Elizabeth squinted to see through the white mist, which swirled around above the even whiter snow. She could also see three small figures up ahead of them—although, in fact they weren't small at all. The closer they got, the larger they seemed: larger even than the reindeer who was carrying her.

"Polar bears!" she cried in excitement. She had heard that such creatures existed, living in the great far north, but of course, she had never seen them. They did not live in Yorkshire, or Durham, or Northumberland, or Scotland. They lived in places where the ice didn't melt and snow fell during summer.

They kept moving toward the bears across snow-covered tundra, until they were not a hundred yards away from them. Elizabeth wondered whether they would retreat at Cary's arrival, but on the contrary, they began moving toward the reindeer and the young girl on his back.

"*These are my friends Sasha and Olga, and their cub Katriana,*" Cary said. "*I know they are very large and fierce looking, but do not be afraid. They are some of the kindest bear-folk I have ever known. And they can speak your tongue. If you are considerate and cordial, they will more than reciprocate your courtesy.*"

Elizabeth clapped her hands. She was very cold, and her teeth were chattering, but she was also very excited. She was going to talk to polar bears!

The three of them approached Cary and bowed, each in turn: the largest among them first, then the other grown bear, and finally the cub. "Welcome to the North Pole. Well, the *magnetic* North Pole," said one of the adults. From the voice, Elizabeth guessed that it was Olga.

"Is there more than one North Pole?" said Elizabeth. She paused, then remembered her manners and hastily added. "Thank you for your welcome! It's so good to meet you!"

"We are glad to meet you, as well," said Sasha. "It isn't often your kind are seen this far north. By your kind, I mean the young of your species. We have, on occasion, seen humans who have come of age. But they only seem interested in hunting our kind, and in slaughtering our brethren, the harp and hooded seals."

Elizabeth lowered her head. "I am sorry."

"We do not blame you," said Olga. "In fact, we are happy to see someone who is *not* interested in hunting and targeting our kind."

Elizabeth smiled shyly, and Olga saw she was shivering. She ambled forward and held out her arms, and the girl stepped forward, hesitant. The large bear put her arms around Elizabeth, and the girl was amazed at how warm she felt inside her arms. It was a real and true bear hug!

Her teeth stopped chattering.

"Is there *really* more than one North Pole?" she said.

The cub laughed merrily, and her father joined in.

"Of course!" Sasha said. "There is one North Pole at the top of the Earth that stays where it is no matter how many years go by. And there is the magnetic North Pole that moves around from year to year. This year, it is here on King Edward Island—at least that's what your kind calls this place. In my youth, it was on a *different* island, a bit to the south of here."

Elizabeth felt confused. "If there are two North Poles, and one is always moving around, how do you know where the *real* North Pole is?"

"It's wherever his Majesty says it is," Sasha answered.

"In fact," said Cary, "at the moment, it's right here."

He nodded his head slightly forward, jostling Elizabeth—who was still on his back—as she tried to keep hold of his antlers.

Once she had steadied herself again, she looked in the direction Cary had indicated and saw a small gatehouse with a gabled roof, alongside which stood a rotating red-and-white column inside a clear vertical cylinder.

"A barber pole?" she said aloud, incredulous.

"Yes, a barber pole. Congratulations for such an astute observation."

Elizabeth scowled behind his back.

"Not just any barber pole, though. This was the first one in the world. His Majesty needed someone to keep that beard of his from

becoming a bird's nest and all that hair from getting in his eyes."

His Majesty? Sasha had said that, too. But Queen Victoria was a lady.

"I told you, we're not in England anymore. Weren't you listening?"

"Well, yes, but that doesn't mean I believe you," she said in her thoughts.

"Even after you saw the North Pole?"

"That's not the North Pole. That's a barber pole at a little building for some imaginary king you made up out of your head."

"You're not the first person to say that about him," Cary scoffed. *"He doesn't care, as long as you're nice."*

Elizabeth didn't think she'd ever been mean to anyone, at least, not so far as she could remember. Even if she had, it wasn't possible to be mean to an imaginary person. Or was it? No, of course, it wasn't! And even if there was a Santa Claus, she wouldn't be mean to him.

"Is there really a barber here?" she said aloud.

"Of course there is!" Olga said, sounding offended. "I am the barber! And the hairstylist. I also do manicures, but I'm a little rusty. King Nicholas doesn't really go in for fancy nails."

Sasha laughed.

But his laughter was cut short by the arrival of a penguin, who came waddling up, then dove onto the ice head-first and slid the rest of the way. He was clearly in a hurry.

"I thought penguins were at the *South* Pole," Elizabeth said.

"*Most of them are*," said Cary. "*But humans seem not to realize that some of* us *like to travel, too. And some of us prefer to relocate if we don't like where we happen to have been born.*"

Elizabeth had never thought of it that way, and she didn't have time to think on it any longer, because the penguin was speaking very quickly and energetically, flapping his little wings in animated fashion to punctuate what he was saying. And what he was saying seemed very disturbing—even if Elizabeth didn't know exactly what he was talking about.

"The Village is being attacked!" he said. "A sky demon has descended upon us! Come quickly! The Village is under siege!"

"Village?" said Elizabeth. "What village?"

But Cary wasn't waiting to hear any more. Before Elizabeth could even say goodbye to the polar bears, he was taking to the sky again, and she found herself holding on to his antlers for dear life.

"What happened?" she said. "Where are we going?"

He didn't answer, perhaps because he was distracted by the sight of dark smoke rising from somewhere just beyond a high snowdrift a fair distance ahead. The clouds had parted and were rapidly fleeing the north wind, revealing the bright moon almost directly overhead. Elizabeth noticed that they were on a cobblestone road now, and realized there was no sign of the high hedgerows that had formed the labyrinth. They were out in the open. On either side of the cobblestone path stood a row of lanterns, oil-flames dancing, spaced at regular intervals until they disappeared behind the snowdrift that lay in front of them.

The smoke was too heavy to be from a chimney. Something was burning.

"*This does not look good.*" Cary's thought wasn't directed at Elizabeth in particular. It was an observation, behind which lay more than a hint of worry.

The girl wondered what was up there.

"*The Village,*" Cary thought, but he was less focused than usual, seeming distracted.

A village at the North Pole. Wait a minute... It couldn't be...

"*Of course it is,*" the caribou said, irritated. "*I thought the name Comet would have given it away. But I know, you don't believe in Christmas. Just because you don't believe in something, that doesn't mean it isn't so.*"

"And just because you believe in something doesn't make it so, either."

Before the reindeer could respond, their attention was drawn to the sky, where a giant winged creature rose from beyond the snowbank. Ascending in front of the moon, it let loose a scream that, even at this distance, was piercing, breathing fire—yes, fire!—in the next moment from its nostrils.

"*A dragon!*" the caribou exclaimed in his thoughts. "*I did not believe they existed!*"

He believed in Father Christmas but not in dragons?

"*I've met Father Christmas, as you call him, but he prefers Nicholas. That would be King Nicholas to you, young woman.*"

Elizabeth snorted. It was bad enough when grown-ups called her "young woman." To hear it from a four-legged furry animal felt downright insulting.

Cary responded by jouncing her a little more than usual, but the thoughts she sensed from him had little to do with her. As they both watched, the dragon soared high, then swooped low again beyond the snowbank. An orange glow flared, followed by a new, dense plume of smoke.

"*It's burning the Village!*" Cary said. "*That beast is burning the Village!*"

And in that moment, something remarkable happened: The girl felt herself being lifted into the air and noticed that Cary's feet were no longer touching the ground! They were moving faster, too. A lot faster. As they rose, the chill air bit savagely at her face. She held on tight to the reindeer's antlers as he banked sharply right, around the snowbank, and the village he had spoken of came into view. It wasn't a large settlement: A few dozen cottages and farms scattered across the snow-covered landscape. But at the center of it was a large clocktower and a village square lined with shops. None of these, she saw, was on fire. The flames were rising from a bit farther on, from a huge complex at the outskirts of the village that looked like a factory of some sort.

The dragon wheeled high in the air, then dove directly toward the complex, fire shooting in straight, yellow-hot streams from his nostrils.

To her horror, Elizabeth realized that the flying caribou (flying caribou!) was headed directly *toward* the dragon, as though intending to intercept it. She closed her eyes tightly and clung to Cary's antler's for dear life. *"This is madness! We'll be killed!"*

"Not if I can help it!"

Cary flew toward the dragon with such speed the still air whistled like a hurricane in the girl's ears. She opened her eyes just enough to see them rising at the last moment before they reached the dragon, which she saw in that same instant was surmounted by a single black-clad rider. In his right hand he held a whip adorned with barbed steel spikes—a whip he was using to flay the dragon's scaled skin mercilessly. Each time he brought the scourge down on the creature's flesh, it screamed in pain and released another stream of molten fire. Elizabeth realized that the great dragon was not acting of its own accord, but was in the thrall of this black rider who had somehow subdued it.

When he was almost on top of the beast, Cary rose

suddenly just above it and kicked violently with his back legs, striking the black-clad rider in the back. Elizabeth heard him shout above the howling wind and saw him topple from his perch and plummet toward the earth. But in almost the same moment, she lost her grip on Cary's antlers and felt his body falling away beneath her. Then she herself was falling, tumbling through the air and downward, ever downward, toward the earth. The last thing she saw was Cary flying nearby. Or was it Cary? She would have sworn she saw *two* flying caribou. Or three. Or four. But maybe her panicked imagination had just multiplied them amid her tumbling-turning fall.

She heard a voice in her head: "*Open your arms!*" and somehow, she complied. She felt a *thud!* against her chest and felt her arms close in front of her, almost by instinct, around a soft and furry something.

Then, she blacked out.

What she awoke to seemed almost as much like a dream as what she'd left behind.

"Where am I?" Elizabeth said, her eyes fluttering open.

She lay on a goose-down bed, wrapped in a warm quilt, in front of a raging fire. It reminded her of the flames she had seen unleashed by the dragon. The poor dragon! It wasn't his fault. The black rider who had tortured him with that awful whip was to blame. "What happened... to the dragon?" She shivered midsentence, and realized she had caught a chill traveling, as she had, through rain and snow and the freezing night.

"Rest, child." A woman with spectacles balanced near the end of her nose and gray-white hair tied back in a tight bun leaned over her, smiling a reassuring smile. The girl did not recognize her, but she felt immediately at ease, as though she had known this woman for as long as she could remember. "You are in our guest chambers. You've been through quite an ordeal, I must say, but there were no broken bones, and once you're warmed up, you should be right as rain.

"As to the dragon, he is recovering, as well. He is being attended. It has been ages since we have seen his kind here, and I fear Lord Nigel is behind his enslavement." A cloud of concern drifted across her eyes.

"Lord Nigel?"

"Yes, my husband's older brother. He has been embittered these many centuries since the crown was bestowed upon my husband, Nicholas. Now, my dear husband is missing, and I fear Nigel used the dragon as a diversion to keep us occupied while he... abducted him."

Elizabeth thought she saw a tear form in the woman's eye, but she couldn't be sure. She was just waking up... or was she still asleep and dreaming?

"Nicholas? As in Saint Nicholas?"

This seemed to brighten the woman's spirits a little,

and she chuckled. "No, dear child," she said. "Saints are dead, and my husband is very much alive... or at least he was the last time I saw him." The cloud of worry returned.

"He is not too fond of titles, but he does rather like the name Father Christmas. His brother prefers a different epithet: Father Time. He seems to think all living things must bend to his will, and now he has set out to prove it."

Elizabeth tried to prop herself up on her elbows, but lay back again when her head began to spin.

"I can't believe any of this," she said, hastily remembering her manners and adding, "no offense intended."

"None taken, child. But if I may ask, how is it that you believe in dragons, but don't believe in my husband?"

"I've met the dragon personally," the girl said.

"And you shall meet my husband, too, if all goes well."

"I pray it will," said Elizabeth, more out of sympathy for the kind old woman than out of any confidence in what she was saying.

"As do I, child."

The woman turned to go, placing a steaming cup of cocoa on a small, circular table beside her.

"Ma'am, one more question, if you please," the girl ventured.

The woman stopped and turned back, waiting.

"How did I survive that fall?"

"Oh, that was Dan. He flew up to catch you when Cary swooped down to save the black rider he had knocked from his perch. Cary won't say it—he's quite ashamed—but he feels terrible that he let you fall off. It is just good fortune that Dan and the others had taken flight at the same time to meet the dragon, and Dan happened to be closest to you when you fell.

"Dan?"

"Some people call him Dancer, because he's so light on his feet, but he prefers Dan. He's very outgoing and doesn't stand on formality, much like my husband." She frowned again, and swallowed hard. "I really must go now, child. It has been a long night, and I fear it will get longer still before it ends."

Elizabeth watched her as she went, then closed her eyes to rest and soon was asleep again.

Chapter Eight

Caravan

The boy thought he might find himself back in the corn maze once again. But, like so many other expectations on this night and in this place, it was simply not to be.

When the mist began to lift and the darkness became a bit less dark, he found himself on a hillside overlooking what appeared to be a settlement. It was not a town, exactly. And it was certainly not a city. It was, rather, a small grouping of structures surrounding a bright bonfire. As he drew closer, he realized, it wasn't a settlement at all, and the structures weren't structures but wooden wagons, each like a little house on wheels, painted in bright colors from red to gold to purple. Half a dozen such wagons were arranged around the bonfire, and he could hear the sound of people laughing and singing at the fireside.

Their song went like this:

I'm a nomad and a vagabond
Now I'm here, and now I'm gone
Adventures come with each new dawn
And I am off to find one

Alex had never seen anything like it.

"I don't think I'm in Iowa anymore," he said, half-aloud.

Pausing for a moment just outside the glowing ring cast by the firelight, he considered, for a moment, bypassing the group, unsure whether to reveal himself without knowing who they were. But his desire to find a way back home outweighed his trepidation. Besides, he had survived an encounter with the Reaper. How much worse could this be?

So, he stepped forward to the edge of the encampment and, when they did not seem to notice him, announced his presence.

"Hello," he said, somewhat meekly.

When there was no response, he repeated, louder, "Hello!"

A young man who'd been sitting by the fire leapt to

his feet, followed by another, and then a third. They seemed to have been taken by surprise, and they moved deliberately toward him like big cats on the hunt, half crouched and muscles tensed. The three appeared as though they had just recently—or were about to—come of age; each of them wore a tunic, tied at the waist by a bright red sash. One of them wore on his head a rich green bandana, the other two sporting similar, flat-topped, wide-brimmed hats. Dark black hair tumbled out from beneath each of their headpieces, though one of the young men had secured his locks in a braid behind him.

"Who's there?" the one in the bandana demanded.

"My name is Alexander," the boy replied, trying to sound important by enunciating his full name.

The young man's eyes seemed to widen, as if in recognition—which was strange, since Alex had never seen him before—then narrowed again. He turned to whisper into the ear of the tall one, who was nearest him, but his voice was still loud enough that Alex could overhear him: "I'm not sure it's him. It could be a trick by Railsback. I didn't think we'd find highwaymen here."

The tall one nodded and whispered back: "I don't know. He seems to match Mama's description, but we've never actually seen him before."

"Better safe than sorry," his companion whispered.

The tall one nodded, then raised his voice and

addressed the boy: "How many are with you, Alexander?" he asked.

"Just me," the boy answered.

"We don't believe you," the tall one said. Then, shouting out into the darkness, he called, "Who goes there?"

The boy noticed that some of the others around the fire had stood and were looking in his direction. Most of them seemed young; some no more than children. Some of the older boys were escorting several girls, each adorned in flowing dresses of many colors, back into the wagons. Alex could not tell exactly how many people were in the encampment, but he guessed there might be about a dozen. They were clearly wary, but not of him; they seemed to believe that he was a decoy or scout, and that others were hiding in the darkness beyond the camp, plotting an ambush.

The boy stepped forward slowly, and the three young men matched his pace as they moved to meet him. The moment he came within a few paces, the one in the bandana leapt forward and roughly took hold of him, grabbing him by both arms and twisting them behind his back. "Rope!" he shouted, and another man emerged out from one of the wagons with a thick double cord that was deftly wrapped and tied around the boy's wrist almost before he knew it was happening.

"Hey!" He pressed briefly against his bonds, but they

only tightened in response, and he quickly realized a struggle would be fruitless. “Let me go!”

The young men ignored him, their eyes instead darting back and forth as they focused on the darkness. “Are you out there, Railsback? We have your spy. Now, show yourself!”

Alex tried to shake their arms off him, but they held him fast. “There’s no one out there!” he protested.

The one holding him bent low near his ear and whispered, “We don’t believe you, boy.”

They stood there for several minutes, scanning the inky murk beyond the encampment for any sign of movement. At last, seeing none, they cursed under their breaths as they began to retreat, dragging Alex with them and pushing him down forcefully at both shoulders to make him sit beside the fire.

“I can’t tell whether he’s the one,” the one in the bandana said.

“Neither can I,” the man with the mustache agreed.

“Maybe he is, but maybe Railsback kidnapped him to do his bidding,” the first man suggested.

They were talking about Alex as though he wasn’t even there. “Who’s Railsback?” he ventured.

All three of them laughed, and the tall man raised a metal tankard to his lips. “You tell us, boy. If you tell us where he is and what he’s up to, we might let you go.”

“Might,” said another, and the three laughed again in

unison.

"He doesn't know." The voice came from behind him, and all three young men turned at the sound of it. It belonged to a woman who had just emerged from one of the wagons. She appeared to be of middle years, with strands of white hair flowing among the golden strands remaining from her youth. Her forehead was high, and her cheeks were soft and round. Had she been smiling, Alex would have seen a single dimple adorn her left cheek—although she was not smiling now. She was not tall; quite the opposite, in fact: She seemed to be scarcely taller than the boy. But at the sound of her voice, the young men all fell silent and nodded their heads toward her in a show of deference.

"He's the one," the woman said curtly. "He doesn't know Railsback."

"As you say, Mama," the tall one said, nodding his head.

"Thank you, Django. You're a good boy." Her thin lips curled upward in a slight smile.

"Yes, Mama," one of the others said.

And the third, more reluctant: "As you say."

The woman bent over and kissed Alex lightly on the top of the head, then sat down, cross-legged, beside him. "You have to forgive my boys," she said. "When we came here, we were attacked by a band of ruffians led by the man named Railsback. We had not been prepared for this, so my boys are wary."

Alex looked more closely at the three young men and noticed bruises around two of their faces, and a recently healed cut above the eye of the third.

"What are you waiting for, Vano? Untie his hands," the woman said. "This is no way to treat our guest."

The one wearing the bandana hurriedly took hold of the rope and had it off of him in an instant.

The woman turned to face him and looked directly into his eyes. "My name is Alamina," she said. "I am the matron of this caravan. These boys here are my sons, Joey, Vano, and Django. Tell me, then, where it is that you have come from?"

"I'm Alex, from Moravia," he answered. "You've probably never heard of it. It's here in Iowa."

Alex thought he saw a flash of recognition in the woman's eyes, but it vanished quickly, and her expression turned inscrutable. "Iowa?" she said.

"Yes," Alex answered. "We're *in* Iowa."

"We are in the Black Forest," Alamina said in a tone that brooked no opposition. "For as long as we have traveled these lands, we have never come upon a town or village called Iowa."

Alex wanted to tell her Iowa wasn't a town, but thought better of it. She seemed as certain of what she was saying as he was of what he knew, and it was pointless to argue in such situations—especially with grown-ups.

"Where are your manners, Joey? Fetch a cup of broth for our friend Alex."

Joey got up quickly and pulled a shallow wooden bowl from a pouch by the fire. He dipped a ladle into an iron cauldron hanging suspended over the fire and spooned some piping-hot liquid into the dish, which he handed to Alex.

"Thank you," he said.

Alamina looked deeply into his eyes as he sipped the broth. "Now, young man, in our culture, it is customary to show kindness to strangers, and it is also customary to repay kindness for kindness." Her voice became suddenly harsher and more insistent. "This is the way of the Romani of the Southern Reach. So tell, me, what do you have that you can use to repay our kindness for welcoming you into our camp?"

Alex blinked twice. He had not expected this. "I... I don't know."

"But surely you have not come to us empty-handed." She seemed to *know* he had something to offer.

Flustered and unprepared for the feeling that he had something the woman wanted, Alex reached into his pocket and put his hand on the only thing there. Before he realized what he was doing, he pulled out the Lou Gehrig baseball card in its plastic sleeve.

He regretted it immediately.

Alamina leaned forward, her eyes widening as if mesmerized. "Ohhh. What have we here?" she said.

"It… it's nothing," Alex stammered.

"Ohhh, but I have never seen anything like it. May I?" She reached out her hand, and Alex noticed the three young men had moved in closer to him. More people were emerging from the wagons, and they were all gathering around him. He glanced this way and that, and thought he might be able to get away, but something told him it was better not to try. Reluctantly, he handed the card to the woman, frantically hoping he might somehow find a way to retrieve it later. The Reaper had told him he would need each of the seven talismans to find his way back home, and without the card, he feared he would be stuck inside this bizarre maze for the rest of his life.

To his surprise, however, Alamina did not seem to be interested in the card itself. She seemed to all but ignore it, glancing at it only briefly before removing it and, instead, marveling at the plastic sleeve!

"I have never seen any material like this!" she said. "If you please, young Alex, I will keep it."

She didn't wait for a response, but handed the sleeve to one of her three sons and returned the card itself to Alex. He hastily returned it to his pocket.

"Now, there's a good lad," said Django, patting him on the head.

He tried not to scowl. He did not like being treated like a child; never mind that he *was* a child.

Alamina smiled, more broadly this time. "That was a test, you know."

The boy's brow furrowed. "A test?"

"Yes, like in school," she said, winking at him, as though she had shared a private joke with him.

He had no idea what it meant.

She continued: "I know the card is a talisman. I trust you, Alex, but I needed to show the others here that you are worthy of that trust: that you are who you appear to be, and that you value the rule of repaying kindness with kindness. It is clear now that you do."

Alex didn't feel too pleased with himself about this. He *had* been all but surrounded. But then, when it came right down to it, he'd always been taught to be kind and show appreciation, especially to his elders, so maybe there was at least a little something to what she was saying. His face brightened.

"Now, since you have shown yourself to be a man of honor..." (his chest puffed out just a little when she called him a man) "...I know I can entrust you with something you will need to complete your journey."

She nodded to Joey, who stood and disappeared inside one of the wagons, each of which had a door at one end and a shallow, curved roof on top. He emerged again a moment later, carrying a square box painted red and gold. Adorned with various designs and swirls, it was inlaid with what appeared to be rubies and sapphires.

When Alamina saw his eyes widen at the sight of the box, she placed two fingers under his chin and turned it toward her. "The box stays here," she said firmly, then smiled when she saw him taking her very, very seriously. "What's inside is far more valuable." She winked again.

This piqued the boy's interest, and when Joey approached and offered him the box, he lost no time in accepting and opening it.

Inside was an ornate compass, set in gold and covered with the same designs that appeared on the box. When he opened it, the needle danced for a moment, then pointed true in one direction.

"North," he said.

"No," Alamina corrected him. "This is a wayfinder compass, the only one ever fashioned, so far as we can tell. All you need to do is set your mind on the place you wish to go, and it will point you in the proper direction."

"Where did the compass come from?" the boy asked, fascinated.

"It has been handed down in our family for generations. When my sister entrusted it to me, she made me promise—as she herself had promised on receiving it—that I should not part with it, no matter what might be offered in return and no matter how great my need might be. It was only to be given to 'the one who would put directions aright and weave the strands of time together as they ought to be.' That's what she told me. And that person, I know, is you."

"That sounds like a big responsibility," the boy said. "I just want to get back home."

"The Compass of the Seventh Kingdom will help you do just that," Alamina assured him. "And it will make everything the way it always should have been. The earth has Seven True Kingdoms, some larger, some smaller, and each separated from one another by the Seven Seas."

Alex didn't know what she meant by that. He had never heard of these Seven Kingdoms. More importantly, though, was the name she had given the compass: It was the same name the Reaper had used for one of the talismans he had listed. He could not believe his good fortune. But then it occurred to him that such fortune would require he grant a kindness in return under the code of the Southern Reach Romani. And he supposed it would have to be something of great value—would she want the Lou Gehrig card after all?

"But I have nothing to offer," he said.

"The fact that you have acknowledged this confirms that I was right about you being worthy of our trust. Yet, as I said, I was charged by my sister to *give* this talisman to the person it was meant for. She knew that what you will accomplish is more valuable even than the talisman itself. That achievement will be the kindness you bestow on us in return."

Smiling, Alex took the compass from the box and placed it in the pocket not occupied by the card. He now had two of the seven talismans the Reaper had said he would need. If the compass could point him in the right direction, he wondered what he would need with the others? Then he reminded himself that the baseball card had likely saved his life in his confrontation with the Reaper, and he decided it was better not to question.

He did not know whether he should ask it to point him directly home, or whether he should request that it take him to one of the other talismans. If he chose the latter course, he wondered which talisman he should seek out next. There was no way of knowing, but his eyesight was keen, so he didn't see the need for spectacles, and he didn't know how to play the flute, so the map made the most sense. It could help him follow the compass, he supposed, letting him know what was between "there" and "here." That way, he could avoid bumping into a mountain or being blocked by a river.

Yes, that made the most sense: He would use the compass to find the map, and then, together, they would allow him to find the rest of them.

He was roused from his thoughts by Alamina, who was speaking once again: "I would invite you to spend the night, but it has been night now for a very long time, a night that will not end until you complete your mission. Nevertheless, you must be tired, so please accept our offer of a place to lay your head. It is Django's turn to stand watch, so you can bed down in his wagon for a few hours—if you can stand the mess!"

Django sent a mock scowl her way, but this evaporated in a moment, giving way to a playful smile. "Of course," he said. "Follow me."

Chapter Nine

Evernight

When Elizabeth woke again, she felt much better. She was still drained, but the chill was gone, having been warmed by the cocoa and the fire. She noticed she was wearing a warm, cotton nightgown, and that her clothes had been set to dry on the hearth.

"We'll keep those here for you if you go out," the woman with the gray-hair bun said. She'd been sitting in a rocking chair by the fireplace, reading a book. "I had some new, warm clothes made up for you so you won't catch another chill." She nodded toward a shallow but broad wicker basket, over the top of which had been lain a heavy wool-and-velvet maroon coat with pearly white buttons down the front.

It looked to be just her size.

Elizabeth's eyes lit up. It was lovely, and it looked so *warm*. She didn't think she ever wanted to be cold again. "Thank you so much!" she said. "Have they found your husband?"

The woman shook her head slowly. "I'm afraid not," she said. "The reindeer have been out looking all over for him, but they've found no sign of him. It doesn't help that it's so dark out there. Even with the full moon, this endless night makes it harder to search than it would be during daylight, and we have no way of knowing where Nigel is keeping him."

"Endless night? Oh, yes." Elizabeth remembered learning that, during the dead of winter, the sun never rose at the North Pole... which still didn't explain how she'd *gotten* to the North Pole in the first place.

"I don't believe we have been properly introduced," the woman said. "My name is Carol Kringle. And I'm afraid 'endless night' is more than just a figure of speech. Usually, the sun begins to wane gradually during the autumn days, but this year, it simply vanished one day and never rose again."

Elizabeth thought about this for a moment. She would have sworn she'd left her home only this very evening, and that the sun had set just an hour or so earlier. Had she really been in the labyrinth for weeks? If so, why did it only seem like hours? And how could she have survived without eating anything until now? It *would* explain how she'd traveled all this way to the North Pole, but it raised more questions than it answered. Time passed differently here; that much seemed clear.

Carol continued her story: "We sent the reindeer out to see what they could discover, and they flew all over the world. It was the same everywhere: Night had fallen, and a veil lay across the heavens, blocking out the sun. There are those who think this is Nigel's doing, but I'm not sure even he could have accomplished this. There are also those who believe that we are trapped in this evernight, and that the sun will never rise again—unless, that is, the right person summons it."

"The right person? You mean your husband?"

"No," she said. "Chris is capable of many things, but this is one thing he cannot do."

"I'm Elizabeth," the girl said. "But I thought you said your husband's name was Nicholas."

"Oh, it is, but as I said, he's not one to be formal. He always preferred his middle name, Christopher, and he usually goes by Chris. Except sometimes, just to needle him, I call him 'Nicky,' she chuckled. "I'm the only one who can get away with that."

She picked up a small China teacup and went to the fireplace, where a teapot hung on an iron bar over the flame. It had just started to give a slow, light whistle.

Carol donned a red oven mitt and removed it, then poured hot water over some tea leaves in the bottom of the cup and brought it over to the girl.

Elizabeth sat up straighter and took it, blowing on it lightly to cool it. "Thank you, Mrs. Kringle," she said.

Carol nodded. "It is my pleasure. Now, as I was saying, the high counselor thinks that only the proper person will be able to bring the daylight back to us. You asked if that person was my husband, and that is precisely what Nigel seems to believe. He thinks that Chris can fly all the way up and remove the veil of darkness. This, I think, is why he abducted my husband: If it's always Christmas Eve, Christmas Day will never come. He has always believed he can stop time, which is why he adopted that self-important title, 'Father Time.'"

For the first time, Elizabeth thought she heard just a hint of bitterness in the woman's voice, but it vanished just as soon as she'd put her finger on it.

"If Christmas never comes, the children of the world, who are his subjects, will never receive their gifts, and they will forget about poor Chris. Then Nigel will be able to ascend the throne and rule in his stead. You'd already forgotten about my husband, I can tell." Her voice didn't seem bitter now; only a little sad. But then her tone brightened. "Maybe we're starting to change at least that much. At least, I hope so."

Carol reached into her pocket and pulled out a small

object. "I'm afraid that when we were getting you out of those wet clothes you were wearing, this fell out of your handbag."

It was the oyster-shaped pocketwatch.

"Oh, thank you!" Elizabeth said, reaching out for it. Carol placed it gently in the palm of her hand "It was a gift... from a friend."

Carol nodded. "And a precious gift it is. It is one of the talismans of time. The high counselor says that only the one who possesses these talismans can restore the world to sunlight and save the day for Christmas." She smiled at her own double-meaning. "Chris knew all about them, and if he were here, I'm sure he'd know just what to do. He always does. Except..." Her voice trailed off, and she shook her head.

"The pocketwatch is still ticking, thank goodness," she said, forcing a smile and changing the subject. "I'm afraid, however, that we also found these in the snow beside you." She stretched forth her soft but wrinkled hand, in which she held a pair of glasses. Elizabeth's glasses. They were in two pieces, broken across the nose-bar; the glass was cracked on one side, and on the other side, was missing completely.

"Oh, dear!" said Elizabeth. She had been so busy taking in everything that had happened to her, that she hadn't noticed her vision was fuzzy! She must have lost her glasses in the fall. "What will I do?" she asked.

Carol put the broken glasses aside and smiled. "We have the world's best craftsmen here at our factory," she said. "And we could have them fashion you a new pair in no time."

Elizabeth brightened.

"But," Carol continued, "I believe we have something better." She stepped over to a rolltop desk in the far corner, from which she retrieved a small wooden case and brought it to the girl. Up close, Elizabeth could see it had been carved with flowing symbols: lettering in a language she could not decipher.

"Elvish runes," Carol explained. "Open it."

Inside the case, Elizabeth found a pair of spectacles, but not just any spectacles. The gold rims contained a pair of lenses, as any spectacles would, but two other lenses attached by moveable arms on either side could be flipped up or down in various combinations.

"Try lowering both lenses on the right side, and the nearest lens on the left," Carol suggested.

Elizabeth did, still looking at the wooden case. The lettering looked much clearer now, but as she studied it, something astonishing took place: It began to swirl before her eyes, the letters coming apart and reforming again, this time in perfectly legible English! "The Spectacles of Samwell Spink," it read.

The girl opened her mouth and barely contained a gasp.

"Who is Samwell Spink?" she said after a moment.

"He was, it is said, the world's foremost optician," Carol replied. "It is rumored that he created these spectacles with magic, as no craftsman, no matter how gifted, has been able to duplicate them. Their gift, if adjusted properly, is to show the wearer all things as they truly are. You can adjust them to focus things close up or at a distance, to be sure, even magnifying them powerfully. At a different setting, they reveal colors beyond the visible spectrum. At still another, they can enable you to see through solid objects; and they can show you how things were in a time past. If adjusted properly, they can be used to translate any script or, perhaps most useful, with a different setting, they can reveal the true nature of anything that stands before you: whether it is faithful or deceitful, noble or malign."

"How do I...?

"Put the two lenses on the left down, over the main lens, but keep both lenses on the right elevated... there, like that."

The girl focused on the older woman, and noticed a warm glow around her. It wasn't just the glow of the fire: It sparkled, almost like flecks of gold swirling in an aura that surrounded her. That must mean she was one of the noble ones. She wondered what someone who was less than noble might look like.

"Guard them well," said Carol. "Like the Pearly

Pocketwatch you hold, it is one of the talismans of time."

Elizabeth nodded.

"How are you feeling?" Carol asked.

Elizabeth stretched her arms over her head and yawned, then took a sip of her tea. It tasted of ginger and elderberry, with a hint of honey. "Much better, thank you. And the tea is very good."

"Isn't it? It's my own special brew. Now, I want to be sure you feel perfectly fine before I ask you a favor. I want to be certain that you feel every bit as fit and healthy as you did when you left home."

"Oh, I feel fine right now," the girl said. "I think I've been lying down too long!" She laughed.

"You are certain?"

Elizabeth nodded.

"Excellent! Because the favor I must ask of you is not a small one, and it should not be agreed to lightly."

The girl leaned forward.

"I know it must have been very scary falling off of Cary like that," Carol said. "I wouldn't blame you if you never wanted to fly again."

Elizabeth thought for a moment. She'd never been particularly scared of heights. Once, when she was younger, she'd even walked out onto the ledge from her window after her Persian cat, Slooferhead, had crawled out there and become too scared to come back in. When she'd fallen off her caribou friend, she hadn't even had time to realize what had happened. She blacked out on the way down, so she didn't even remember most of it. What she did remember had been exhilarating.

"Not at all," she said finally. "I would *love* to fly again."

"That is the favor I must ask you," Carol said, her expression turning serious. It was a rare look for her. "It is my hope that the Spectacles of Samwell Spink will help you find my Nicky."

Elizabeth smiled. She was eager to be of help. "Where is Cary going to take me?" she said, expectantly.

Carol shook her head. "You won't be going with Cary. We'll need someone who can provide more light to help you see. Reindeer don't have glowing red noses, you know! We need something as bright as the flame in my fireplace to light up the night and show you where to look."

As bright as flame? What could she mean...? Then it dawned on her.

"The dragon?!"

Carol nodded. "Dreqnir was grateful to us for freeing him, having been in the thrall of Nigel and his lieutenant, Tar Kidron. Dragons are magically bound to a single human when they come of age, and Tar Kidron had bound Dreqnir to himself. When we captured him, he renounced his allegiance to Nigel and agreed to relinquish this bond to another. I would like that person to be you."

"He seemed so cruel, whipping the poor dragon like that," said Elizabeth. "Why would such a heartless person change so suddenly?"

"Being our North Pole Village has a certain... effect on people, which is why Nigel never comes here or permits any of his followers to do so. Nicky calls it the spirit of Christmas."

Elizabeth had to admit she was right. The fire was not the only or even the greatest source of warmth in this place. She felt more at ease, more thankful, and more open-hearted than she could ever remember feeling.

Chapter Ten

Likho's Realm

Sleeping in Django's wagon was an adventure in its own right. Colorful clothes, scarves, and tapestries were strewn all around the place; the young man kept a blue macaw perched on a wooden post in one corner, and a rambunctious monkey jumped and bounced around, sometimes leaping at the macaw, which flew away from him in a flurry of wings and feathers.

Sleeping was a challenge, at best, and the hours he spent in the lumpy mattress that passed for a bed involved mostly tossing, with a good bit of turning thrown in for good measure.

When he awoke, it was still dark as ever.

"Up with you!" Django said good-naturedly as he

shooed the monkey away from a half-eaten apple—Alex didn't know whether the missing bites had wound up in Django's tummy or the primate's. The macaw flew over and landed on his shoulder. "It's time to continue our journey!" Django said.

"*Our* journey?"

"Yes!" He smiled and reached down, grabbing Alex by his collar and pulling him to his feet.

"Hey!"

"Mama insisted that one of us go along to keep you safe. She said you're too important to let anything happen to you. You don't look so important to me, but what do I know? If Mama wants me to go, I go."

Alex wasn't exactly in a position to argue, being a lot smaller than Django. Nor was he particularly bothered by the prospect of having some company on the road. With the exception of Mr. Rrawk and the scarecrow, who hadn't been with him long, and the kobold "king," who had hardly been a friendly companion, he'd been traveling by himself long enough. Django was the youngest (but also the tallest and most vocal) of the three brothers he had met, but was a few years older than he was, which might be a good thing, too. He knew these woods, and he supposed he knew some other things that could prove helpful, as well—even if those "things" didn't include keeping a tidy wagon.

Vano, who had taken Django's watch beside the fire,

sat close to it, warming his hands and poking it occasionally with a long stick. Sparks rose from it whenever he did, darting about in the darkness like fireflies.

Django gave him a brief wave of acknowledgement, which Vano returned, but no words passed between them as the boy and the young Romani man set out from the camp, each carrying a small oil lantern and a small pack stuffed with provisions.

"Don't you want to say goodbye to your mother?" Alex asked.

Django laughed. "She'll be coming with us," he said.

Alex, however, saw no sign of her, and Django threw his head back in mock frustration. "Have you never heard of a crystal ball?"

The boy had, indeed, heard of such things, but he had been sure they were nothing more than props used by fortune tellers and vendors at the state fair.

"She'll be able to see us whenever she wants," Django explained. "All she'll have to do is take a peek inside the old misty orb."

Alex wasn't sure whether to believe him or not. Django had a way of speaking that always left some doubt as to whether he was on the level or having a joke at the boy's expense. It could be... unsettling.

"Which way is that thing telling you to go?" Django asked, referring to the compass.

"Oh," the boy said. "Right." He pulled out the compass and watched as the needle danced wildly this way and that.

"For it to work, you have to decide where you want to go," Django prompted.

"I want to find the Map of Gildersleeve," Alex said firmly, addressing the compass itself more than his companion.

The needle immediately stopped dancing and settled in to a clear, unwavering position. It didn't point along the pathway leading away from the camp, but rather, into a dense thicket of trees at the edge of the clearing.

Django shook his head. "We can't go that way," he said. "There is no path, and the river lies that way. It's broad and runs fast for miles in both directions; there is no way to ford it. Besides, those are the lands of Likho." He repeated, more firmly: "No, we cannot go that way."

"This is why we need the map," Alex grumbled, still looking toward the place where the needle was pointing. It seemed just as convinced that they should go that way as Django was that they shouldn't. "Who's Likho?"

"The Guardian of the Forest," Django answered, taking hold of the boy's wrist and trying to pull him along on the path. "Likho is a trickster. He will deceive and misdirect you, especially if you hunt or even scorn the creatures of his forest. But if you enter there, you *must* hunt if you are to survive, for Likho has charged the trees and bushes there not to produce any fruit that can be eaten. There is no winning with Likho. You will become hopelessly lost in there if you go that way. He will make sure of it.

Alex broke free of his grip. First the kobold, and now Django: Everyone seemed to think they could force him to go where *they* wanted him to go. He had his own ideas, and the more others tried to dissuade him from pursuing them, the more fiercely he tended to cling to them. He was already lost, and he had been told the compass could be trusted. To use it properly, he needed that map, and if the compass said the map lay in *that* direction...

"I'm going," he announced.

He didn't wait for Django to respond to him, but instead took off running in the direction the needle pointed.

The tall young man had no choice but to run after him, following the boy's flickering lantern light.

"Wait!" he called, but almost before the word was out of his mouth, Alex had disappeared into the trees ahead of him. He was fitter and had longer legs, but by the time those legs had caught up to the boy, they were far enough into the forest that it was hard to tell which was the proper way out. Their lantern light flickered against trees that had already shed their autumn leaves, rising up with jagged, forking branches in a dense tangle that all but blocked out the dark night sky.

The only clear sense of direction was provided by the compass, and it was still pointing, insistent, toward the same destination.

The two stood side by side, both out of breath from the chase.

"I told you, we *can't* go that way!" Django said.

"The compass says we have to," the boy responded.

Django sighed. "Very well. But if we starve to death in here, I'm going to strangle you." He seemed extremely serious about this, despite the absurdity of strangling someone who was already dead.

"If the river gets in our way, we can just follow it until we find another way across."

"Mama says that river is magical, and I told you, there's no way to cross for miles! I might be able to make it that far, but you'll get tired, and I'll have to carry you. Then I'll get tired and we'll both just end up dying here, if Likho doesn't find us first."

"Likho, Likho, Likho!" Alex mocked. "I'm not scared of your silly stories."

Django shook his head. "You'll see," he said, resigned. Then, more to himself in a whisper: "You'll be sorry."

Nevertheless, they followed the compass forward, except where it pointed them directly at some obstacle like a large tree or a rock that they had to go around. They spoke little as they traveled, the normally talkative Django having settled into a glum resignation at having been overruled by a young boy. As skeptical as he'd been about this Likho character, Alex had to admit that Django had been right about one thing: Not much fruit grew here, and that which he saw was either barbed or shriveled or an unappetizing gray. In fact, almost everything was gray or black here in the woodland, and it wasn't just the night that made it appear so. The Black Forest, Alamina had called it, and the name was certainly apt.

Now and then, an owl hooted mournfully in the distance, or a squirrel scuttled across their path. Once, a buck appeared almost directly in front of them, antlers majestic and dark eyes flashing in their lantern light. It looked at them directly for a few seconds, then bounded away into the trees. Moss grew on those trees, and mushrooms sprang up from the forest floor. Beetles crawled up and down tree trunks, and earthworms burrowed their way into the ground beneath their feet.

They occasionally heard a low, lumbering-grumbling sound, like someone or something very heavy traipsing through the woods, accompanied by something that seemed halfway like a groan and halfway like a growl.

"Likho," Django said simply whenever they heard it, and when it sounded closer, Alex could see him tense his muscles.

Whatever it was, the sound *was* disconcerting. The boy thought it might be a bear, which was far more worrisome than some imaginary forest guardian. But then, they came upon some tracks that didn't look at all like they'd been made by a bear. The footprints looked human, but were perhaps three times as large, with impressions around the edges that seemed to have been made by leaves.

"Likho," Django said again. And the next time the sound came, closer still, he ducked quickly behind a tree, pulling Alex along with him.

"If you see him, do not look directly at him. Always look *past* him," the young man said. "If you meet his eyes, they will beguile you, and you will be at his mercy."

A moment later, the sound stopped, and the two of them stepped tentatively out from behind the tree. Django looked this way and that, and the boy followed his eyes, but neither of them could see far in the dim lantern light. After a moment, when the strange sounds appeared to have gone silent, Alex glanced again at the compass, and they set out again in the direction the arrow was pointing.

Before they had gone a dozen steps, though, an owl swooped down from some unseen branch, flying almost directly in front of them. Almost without thinking, the pair instinctively leaped to one side in tandem. But instead of landing on solid ground, they found themselves in an abrupt and unexpected descent, through a blanket of leaves that had masked a thin layer of loosely bound rope-netting.

It tangled them up in it as they fell, slowing their journey downward and, eventually, catching them before they could hit anything hard in the darkness below. It was a good thing, too, because they had fallen for some distance. The netting had caught their lanterns, too—which had somehow, fortuitously, remained lit during their tumble—but their glow was not enough to illuminate whatever lay beneath them, save for a single rock outcropping just a few feet down.

Before they could take any further account of their surroundings, they heard the sound of sawing, a jagged-toothed blade scraping back and forth against... the rope that was holding them up!

A moment later, the rope gave way.

"Ooof!" Django landed on the outcropping below them with a thud, the impact knocking the air from his lungs.

"Ouch!" said Alex, landing beside them.

Django leapt to his feet and grabbed his lantern, which was teetering at the edge of the outcropping, before he lost it over the precipice. Alex's lantern was nowhere to be seen. A few pebbles fell toward them from above, bounced off the rock ledge, then disappeared into the chasm below. If they made a sound where they landed, it was too far down for the pair to hear it.

Alex looked upward, but it was too dark outside to tell the difference between the blackness of the pit and the night beyond. And he knew they'd fallen too far to climb back out, even if they were sure they could find handholds. Someone might as well have sealed them in.

"Nice work, magic compass," Django spat. And he really *did* spit, off over the edge, in disgust. "I wish Mama had never given you that thing."

The compass needle, as if in answer, spun three times around and pointed directly at Django, accusingly.

"You better watch what you say," Alex said. "You said your mother would be watching us." He had intended it as sarcasm, but Django seemed to take it so seriously he put his hand over his mouth and gazed upward apologetically. He actually appeared convinced his mother *was* watching them.

His head snapped forward again, however, at the sound of something scuttling toward them. It wasn't the sound of footsteps, exactly, but a shuffling and skittering in the darkness that grew gradually louder until the thing that had been making the sound appeared at the edge of the lantern light.

The creature before them was very small: less than a foot long, Alex was sure. Almost half its size seemed contained in a pair of giant hands equipped with very long nails. It had a long nose, too, and the whiskers at the end of it twitched in keen interest as it sniffed the air. Its eyes were so small that the boy couldn't even be sure it had any, hidden as they were behind the layer of soft brown fur that covered it.

"A mole," said Django, clearly unimpressed.

The mole turned toward the sound of his voice.

"Not just any mole," it quipped. "Xander Molander the Third, at your service."

Moles talked too? The boy had spent his entire life thinking that only people knew how to speak. Well, there were a couple of exceptions. Parrots, for example. And he *had* heard that crows like Mr. Rrawk could mimic human speech, but not that they could actually form words based on original thought.

"The third, eh?" said Django. "What happened to the first two?"

Xander Molander the Third shrugged. "Not sure. We're not a close family. But I can tell you one thing: They didn't get caught in one of Likho's traps. Haha!"

Likho again. Who *was* this Likho?

"It's his fault," Django objected, pointing at the boy. "He insisted on entering Likho's realm. I told him it was a bad idea."

"It doesn't look like he listened to you," the mole said. "What did he do? Tie you up? Intimidate you? Threaten your mama if you didn't go with him?"

Django's face contorted into the kind of expression someone makes when he snarls, although he didn't make any sound. Alex was sure he was biting his tongue. He remembered the young man had said it wasn't a good idea to scorn the creatures of Likho's forest, and he guessed Django was trying his best to avoid doing just that.

"Can you take us to this Likho?" the boy suggested.

"Very good! Very good, my young friend," the mole responded. "That is precisely what I am here to do."

Chapter Eleven

Tree-Man

Xander led Alex and Django through a twisting, turning series of passageways that seemed even more daunting than the corn maze itself. Django's lantern provided precious light, but the mole didn't seem to need it. He appeared to know exactly where he was going, and never once hesitated where the passageway split in two or more directions, always plunging ahead into the darkness without a second thought.

The mole may have been small, but fortunately for the two human visitors, the passages were not. The ceilings were easily high enough for them both to stand at their full height, and all signs suggested that they'd been here for a very long time: The stone path beneath their feet wasn't dusty, but had been worn smooth by time and perhaps hundreds of feet. The path seemed to be rising gradually as they moved forward, an impression confirmed by the appearance of tree roots pushing down through the ceiling.

Then, however, it leveled off and opened out a few moments later into a large cavern. Water fell in drips and drops, splashing rhythmically into pools on the smooth rock floor. But Alex and Django barely noticed this, transfixed as they were by something else that was happening directly in front of them: The roots were moving, burrowing deeper into the cavern and pushing outward against the earth of the ceiling, causing bits of dirt and rock to cascade down like solid rain. Alex dropped to one knee instinctively, bending forward and putting his arms up over his head. For a moment, it seemed the entire ceiling might collapse. But then, he realized that the roots were creating a hole in the ceiling, which turned out to be the opening to a tunnel from overhead.

Through that tunnel could be heard the same lumbering-grumbling sound Alex remembered from the forest above.

It was getting louder.

"Likho," Django breathed.

"Yeah, I know," Alex wanted to say. He wished Django would stop saying that, in part because it was annoying, but even more so because the way he said it was spooky, as though he was trying to creep him out. Whatever his purpose, it was getting old—but Alex was too young to be sarcastic about it. Whatever was making that sound *was* scary, regardless of what Django might choose to call it. He was far more worried about what it looked like and, more to the point, what it might do. He didn't have to wait long to find out.

The rumbling grew louder still, and a moment later, more earth fell from the opening in the ceiling. Then, something emerged. It was large and bulky, and it looked like a giant man, but also like a tree. His mouth was almost entirely obscured behind a long, scraggly beard, which tumbled down across his chin and down his chest, the strands appearing more like thin and twisted roots than human hair. So thick was it, that it was difficult to see whether he wore anything underneath it. His eyebrows looked like cones from a pine tree that had yet to open, and his head was crowned by what looked like branches in the form of antlers, surmounting a forehead and glazed gray eyes.

Those eyes stared at the two young humans, without moving. They didn't appear to be looking for anything, so much as they seemed to be staring at something they knew was already there. What that something was, the mouth beneath that scraggly beard wasn't saying. At least not yet.

Alex looked sidelong at Django, who had dropped to one knee and bowed his head before the strange figure, which stood perhaps four times the height of a man, its head touching the ceiling of the voluminous cavern. Django reached up with one hand, placed it on Alex's shoulder, and pulled him forcefully down until he, too, was kneeling.

Alex brushed the hand aside, stood up, and dusted the dirt off his knees. He had faced the Grim Reaper, he reminded himself, and this figure, no matter how imposing, couldn't be as fearsome as all that.

Xander was shaking his mole-head vigorously back and forth. The boy ignored him.

"My name is Alexander, sir," he said, noticing that his voice shaking more than he wanted to allow. "What do you want us for?"

There was a rumbling low in the stomach of the creature—do trees have stomachs? Alex asked himself—and the boy noticed for the first time that the noise sounded faintly like the name Django had been uttering: "Lurheeeko." The middle syllable sounded like wind being pushed out of a bellows. Then it repeated what the boy himself had said: "What do you want us for?"

"I don't want you," the boy said plainly. "I just want to get home."

"I see," Likho said, then fell silent.

"We humbly seek passage through your lands," said

Django, still kneeling. "We have harmed nothing living here. You have our word."

"Of course, you have not," Likho replied. "You know the consequence for doing so. But tell me: What is your destination?"

Alex reached into his pack and produced the Compass of the Seventh Kingdom. "We are following the needle."

Impossibly fast, a gnarled tree-hand flashed forward and snatched at the compass. Before the boy's young reflexes could close his fingers around the object, it was no longer in his hand.

Likho lifted it up to examine it closely.

"Ah, yes. I know of this artifact," he said. "The Compass of the Seventh Kingdom. Are you aware that artificial mechanisms are forbidden in my realm?"

The boy heard Django inhale nervously.

"I will be keeping this," said Likho, his voice flat. "And you will leave my realm immediately."

"But we can't find our way out!" Alex protested, his voice rising. "I need that!"

"That is not my problem," Likho answered. Then, almost as an afterthought: "The compass will do you no good, in any case, without the map."

"Yes!" Alex blurted out. "The Map of Gildersleeve. That's what we're looking for!"

The glazed look on Likho's face lifted for a moment,

and the light of mischief danced briefly in his eyes, then was gone. "I have it," he said almost offhandedly, then reached into his beard and pulled it out! "And I might have given it to you if you hadn't broken the rules and brought that mechanical instrument into my realm."

Alex shook his head. Without the compass, the map would do him no good. And without the map, the compass would only get him so far. The compass had directed him this way. If he'd had the map before, maybe it would have shown him a way *around* Likho's realm, but that was impossible if Likho himself had the map!

This was hopeless.

Django stood up and addressed the tree-man: "If I may..."

"Silence!" Likho thundered in a loud and echoing rumble. "I was not speaking to you."

Django fell back to one knee and bowed his head again. Alex took two steps backward. The mole, he noticed, was nowhere to be seen.

Likho lowered his voice, bending down over Alex so that his root-beard brushed against the boy's face.

It tickled.

"What if I told you that there was, in another place and time, a girl who is hopelessly lost, just as you are?"

Alex blinked and raised his eyebrows.

"Now," the tree-man continued, "what if I told you that she needed the map and compass just as you do, and that she could never find her way home without it?"

Alex's eyes widened.

"Who...?"

"That is not important," Likho said flatly.

Django raised his head, although he did not stand this time, and spoke again: "If this girl is in another place and time, as you say, how do you know of her if you never venture forth from your realm?"

Alex expected the tree-man to respond with another thunderous objection, but instead, he turned to face the young Romani, that mischievous twinkle dancing in his eyes once again—if only ever so briefly. "I said, 'what if,'" he pointed out. "Nevertheless, it is a good question, so I will indulge it. You must remember that I am part tree, and trees are very long-lived, so if that 'different time' were a century behind us, I would have witnessed it already. As to how I might see such things without leaving my own realm, I will pose a question of my own: How can your own mother see you here, though she has never left your caravan?"

"A crystal ball?" Django breathed. He seemed surprised, but also, strangely, worried.

"Nothing so mundane," Likho rumbled. It sounded vaguely like a laugh. "There are many ways of seeing, most of which you know nothing of. I merely cited your mother's way as an example. Suffice to say that time and space are not so constant as you humans seem to think, and that on this, All Hallows' Eve, the veil between the worlds of past and present, here and there, is uncommonly thin. It is a simple matter to see across miles and across decades, if you know how.

"However," he continued, turning his attention back to Alex, "if you do not succeed in finding your way home, the veil will become a barrier, severing past from present and present from future. There will be chaos, and the entire world will be trapped in this maze of yours forever."

The entire world. The words echoed in the boy's young mind.

The boy looked at Likho, trying to figure out what the tree-man was up to. It seemed unbelievable that the fate of all the world depended on him finding his way home. But if it were true...

"Why not give me the map and compass, then?"

Likho straightened his back and rose again to his full height. "Because," he said, "you broke the rules."

"I didn't *know* the rules!" he protested.

"That doesn't matter," Likho answered. "But, given the gravity of your present predicament, I might be convinced to give you this"—he sneered—"mechanical instrument, and the map you seek, as well. But know this: that in doing so, you will condemn an innocent little girl to be lost forever in a labyrinth."

Django whispered earnestly in his ear: "This is a

stroke of luck!" he said. "Likho *never* violates his own rules. You *must* take him up on this offer. It will not come again."

Alex turned to him and whispered back. "What about the girl?"

"She is only one person. What is the fate of one person when measured against the entire world?"

The boy thought for a moment. Something about this was not quite right. It didn't make sense that Likho would refuse to give him the map and compass—then suddenly change his mind. The tree-man appeared to have known about this girl all along; if she needed the two talismans so badly, why hadn't he simply given them to her himself? Or, if the entire world depended on him finding his way home, why did he even mention the girl?

Likho appeared to have been reading his thoughts. "Because," he said, "the decision must be yours. I only took the talismans for safekeeping, to guard them from him." He nodded toward Django.

Django stood up ramrod straight. "Me?" he said, looking shocked.

"Yes, you," the tree-man said, a hint of disdain in his deep voice. "Do not feign innocence. I have seen your kind before. Young men who believe they know everything, when they have experienced next to nothing. Tell me you were not indignant that your mother should have bestowed the compass upon a stranger. It has been in your family for... how many generations?"

Django shook his head vigorously. "No! I..."

"It doesn't matter," Likho continued. "What matters is that you and your ancestors have long used the compass to enrich yourselves. It has guided you to treasures forgotten in the forest; to naïve travelers you might trick out of their fortunes; to roe deer and boar, to hare and pheasant that you might slaughter and feast upon them!" His voice grew fierce and angry as he spoke this last, rising from a low rumble to a roar.

Django cowered before him. "But I swear, none of those creatures were taken in your realm!" His voice quavered. "I swear it on my honor."

"Honor?" Likho shouted. "You think it honorable to use the Compass of the Seventh Kingdom to line your pockets and take innocent lives? Are those lives less worthy because they live beyond my realm?"

Django was silent. He did not know what to say.

"Is he telling the truth?" said Alex. "Were you really going to take the compass from me?"

Django shook his head vigorously, but it was Likho who spoke, his voice dropping again from its indignant fury. "He does not matter," the tree-man said. "His mother will deal with him. *She*, at least, has honor, and he appears to have forgotten that she was watching him, though I did do him the courtesy of reminding him..."

That explained why he'd sounded worried.

"He does not matter," Likho repeated. "What matters is your decision: Will the talismans go with you, or shall I send them to the girl?"

The boy thought, and thought again. He turned the matter over in his head, then spun it 'round and pulled it inside out. He still could not quite believe that the fate of the entire world might rest upon his shoulders. But there was something about knowing that someone else, a girl perhaps close to his own age, might be lost forever if he did not help her. Could he live with himself if he allowed that to happen? He decided, at the end of all his thinking, that he could not.

"Give them to her," he said.

Django gasped.

"Are you certain?" asked the tree-man. "If I do this, I will not be able to get them back."

The boy nodded.

"Very well." Likho waved his hand, and the map and compass both vanished.

Alex's shoulders slumped. He was more certain, once he uttered the words, that he had done the right thing, but with that certainty came the realization that the chances of finding his own way home had almost certainly slipped through his fingers.

Likho leaned down again close to him, and his tone, for the first time, seemed sympathetic. "I know this forest better than my own beard," he said, stroking the tangled strands with a gnarled, woody hand. "And I can direct you to one of the other talismans, which lies within my realm. It is the Flute of Pan's Third Daughter, and with it, you may yet find your way back home."

The boy's face brightened. "Why didn't you say so?" he asked.

"I had to be sure that you were worthy," Likho answered.

Alex was starting to get tired of all these tests. First the scarecrow, then Alamina, and now the tree-man. The least they could do would be to *tell him* he was being tested. The way things were going, he worried he might fail one of these tests eventually and be stuck here for all eternity.

Likho's voice, however, was reassuring. "You made the right choice, boy," he said. "I spoke the truth when I said the girl could not get home without the talismans. But I never said it was impossible for you."

The boy's eyes grew wide as he remembered what the tree-man had said. He had not understood it at the time; now, he did.

"But do not think the road ahead will be easy," the tree-man continued. "Without the map and compass, your path ahead is much more difficult. Indeed, you will not be able to find your way back alone; you will need to rely on the heart of another. If that heart is pure, and its owner wise, you may yet find your way home, and the world may yet be saved. But if not..."

He left the rest unsaid.

Chapter Twelve

Stew and Cider

The dragon seemed far larger up close than he had from a distance in the sky.

Dreqnir was curled up outside Chris and Carol's home, because he couldn't have fit inside. As Elizabeth looked at the village around her, she was certain he couldn't have fit inside any of the other buildings, either. She would have felt bad for him, lying outside in the freezing polar air, had it not been for a warm quilt, as thick as the wall of a house, draped over him so completely that it covered everything from the top of his head to the tip of his tail.

Carol told her that Chris' staff of workers had sewn it in just a few hours; they were known not only for their quick work, but for its quality. Elizabeth imagined that no one would have been cold under that quilt. Only Dreqnir's nose peeked out from beneath it, with puffs of steam escaping like balls of cotton with each new breath. Occasional sparks flew out, as well, and Elizabeth couldn't tell whether the steam was being formed by the dragon's breath condensing in the cold air or whether it was actually smoke issuing forth from within. She imagined the inner fire helped keep him warm, as well.

Elizabeth had no such natural source of warmth, and she shivered a little in the cold, even underneath the warm wool-and-velvet coat Carol had given her. Swirls of golden-brown hair peeked out from underneath a matching woolen cap that fit snugly over her head, complete with side flaps that shielded her ears from the winter cold. Matching gloves warmed her hands. On the bridge of her nose rested the Spectacles of Samwell Spink, which were attached by a tight band around the back of her head to ensure that they wouldn't fall off again.

Dreqnir lifted his head as she approached.

"Hello, Dragon," the girl said.

"Dreqnir," the dragon said.

"I beg your pardon, Dreqnir," Elizabeth said, smiling.

Dreqnir smiled back, and Elizabeth's smile vanished as she stared wide-eyed past two parallel rows of gleaming, knife-point teeth. Had she wished to, she could have stepped into that mouth with plenty of room to spare; the dragon would have had no difficulty in swallowing her whole. Past the tongue and toward the back of Dreqnir's throat, the girl could see the faint golden glow of molten fire shining up from his belly.

"Dreqnir Dreqsson Flameblast," the dragon announced, raising his head proudly. "Forty-fifth of his name and Duke of the Northern Reach."

Elizabeth recovered her wits as questions flooded her head. Dragons could speak? Dragons had dukes? She'd never even *seen* a dragon before; she'd thought they existed in myths and fables.

"I do not wish to be rude," the girl said, "but how many of you are there?"

"That," said Dreqnir, "is a secret. If I were to say that we are few, men would hunt us, believing our teeth and scales to be rare and, therefore, valuable. If I were to say that we are many, men would fear our numbers and train their weapons on us whenever we might appear. Knowledge is power, little one, and men cannot be trusted to use it wisely."

It was here that Carol spoke up: "Not all humans are foolish and self-centered. If they were, who would there be to celebrate Christmas? Without nice children to reward with stockings full of gifts each winter, poor Nicky would have nothing to do! He would have no reason to make any toys."

The dragon sniffed. "Nice children can turn into very mean grown-ups," he said. "Tar Kidron was a nice little boy, once upon a time. He was 'nice' when I bound myself to him. But once-upon-a-times become second thoughts as years move past us, and second thoughts become foul deeds. The little boy I knew would never have done the things he has done."

"There are other little boys," said Carol, "and little girls"—she smiled at Elizabeth—with good hearts..."

"That can just as easily be corrupted."

Carol nodded. "What if I were to tell you that the fate of Christmas and the world itself rested on the shoulders of just such a little girl?"

Dreqnir shifted his gaze to Elizabeth, and appeared to be eyeing her more closely. "Then I would pray to all of my ancestors in Dreqinholl that she completes her task before she can be corrupted." He paused, then turned back to Carol and said: "How is it, exactly, that you expect her to save Christmas... and the world?"

Carol shook her head. "I don't know. The high counselor doesn't know, either. I know my Nicky would be able to tell us. But Nigel is holding him somewhere. That is why we need you to find him."

"That, and you miss your husband," Dreqnir said with a laugh.

Carol responded with a sad half-laugh of her own. "And that, yes."

Snow began falling then, flakes fluttering down and settling on the dragon's nose. He curled his bottom lip upward and blew at them, then shook them off.

A few feet away, a street lantern flickered and went out.

"It's getting harder and harder to keep them lit," Carol remarked. "The evernight is getting darker."

"It's like a heavy veil is falling," the girl said.

"Yes," said Carol, her head bowed. "Just like that."

She looked up again at the dragon. "We need your help, Dreqnir Dreqsson Flameblast," she said solemnly. "Will you allow yourself to be bound to Elizabeth? Will you help her find my Nicky?"

But before he could answer, Elizabeth said: "I don't want Dreqnir to be like a slave. I don't want him to feel like he has to do what I say, the way Tar Kidron made him burn your village and fight with Cary. I never want anything like that for him."

Dreqnir curled back his lips. It looked like a grimace, but the girl saw a smile dancing in his eyes.

"The bond is not like that," he said reassuringly. "It is a bond of trust. It only becomes a burden when that trust is abused. That is what Tar Kidron did. I will *never* be *anyone*'s slave again," he said firmly.

Carol's expression was downcast, but then the dragon continued: "Your concern for me is noted, little one, and it is welcome. Because of it, yes, I will consent to be bound to you."

Elizabeth thought she heard Carol breathe a sigh of relief.

"Are you sure?" the girl said.

The dragon nodded and leaned forward, laying his head on the ground very close to Elizabeth. For the first time, she noticed something about him: A stone redder than a ruby was embedded in his scales, gleaming with a starburst on his forehead just above and between his eyes. She pointed, then pulled her hand back, realizing it was impolite. "What is that?" she asked.

"It is my heart, little one. A dragon's heart is what some humans might call his third eye. It sees inward and is connected by a cord to the center of his mind. For a dragon, heart and mind are always unified, unlike in you humans, for whom they often seem to be at war. Go ahead and take it."

"Take it? But..."

"If we are to be bonded, you must take it and place it next to your own heart. It is how we will communicate our deepest wishes and most profound dreams with one another. It is how I will know your intentions and how you will know mine."

The girl had to climb on Dreqnir's nose to reach the heart-gem, and he chuckled a low dragon chuckle as her small feet tickled his shiny scales. When she reached down toward the heart, it seemed to glow more brightly, as though the dragon fire within him had enveloped it with red-gold aura. She was amazed at how easily it came loose in her hand, and at how warm it felt, even in the frigid polar chill.

"We can sew it into the lining of your coat," Carol suggested, and the dragon nodded in agreement.

"We fly in the morning," Dreqnir said.

"But first, a hearty meal and a good long sleep are in order!" Carol said.

As if on cue, four villagers appeared, all dressed in the same kind of warm woolen coat that Carol and Elizabeth both wore. Slender and lithe, they were shorter than average but seemed, despite this, uncommonly strong. This was evident, because each of the four held one end of a sturdy rope, the other end of which was tied to a massive wooden bowl of... stew! It was as deep and wide as a tiny house, and steam rose in wisps and curls from the center of it.

The girl wondered that such a thing might have been simply lying around, waiting to serve the next dragon who happened to pop in for supper. It was too big, its rim too high, for any other creature to make use of: Not even the tallest draft horse could have reached its chin and muzzle over the edge. Then, she remembered that Carol had told her the Kringles employed the world's best craftsmen at their factory.

"Are they your craftsmen?" she said, pointing to the

four.

Carol smiled and nodded. "A few of them. They are from a race spread across the northern lands and polar reaches. The Danes call them the Nisse, and the Finns know them as the Keijukainen. In Iceland, they are the Alfur. In an earlier age, they ruled these lands peacefully, and their realm stretched from Siberia across to the Baltics and as far as Hudson's Bay here in the New World. But while their realm was vast, their numbers were never many, and when your race, the race of man, began to multiply, they moved north with dreams of conquest."

Dreqnir looked up after loudly slurping up a mouthful of stew. "The race of man," he scoffed.

Carol looked briefly at the dragon, and the girl saw a tinge of sadness in that look.

She continued: "The Vikings in Scandinavia and the Mongols in Siberia drove northward to stake their claims, but rather than defending their land, the Alfur withdrew, much as Dreqnir's dragonfolk did. They built this village here, and helped us with our task of crafting the gifts Nicky delivers to good children every year. In days of old, when there were far fewer children on the earth, he crafted all these gifts himself, but as more children came into the world, their help was more than welcome!"

"How old *are* you?" the girl blurted out, then clapped

a hand over her own mouth on realizing the temerity of the question.

Carol laughed aloud. “I don’t discuss my age,” she said, but did not seem offended. Instead, there was a light dancing merrily in her eyes. “Let’s just say that I’m old enough to know things that the Alfur’s ancestors had long forgotten.”

“But not my ancestors,” Dreqnir said. “Their lore is inscribed there.” He tapped a long, sharp toenail against the heart-gem Elizabeth held, then took a long, deep draught from the bowl of soup.

“Ah! You should try it,” he said to Elizabeth. “It’s very good.”

The snow had stopped falling by the next morning, although it didn’t seem like morning, of course, because it was still dark. It was not *quite* as dark as it had been before, however, because the clouds had cleared away. They had been peeled back to reveal a velvet-black sky, inset with tiny ice-blue diamond stars twinkling merrily overhead.

Elizabeth climbed into a sleigh-shaped seat, which the Alfur had crafted to fit perfectly on Dreqnir’s back. And she, in turn, fit perfectly into the seat, which had been designed to her specifications. Leather straps held her snugly but comfortably in place, and an invisible barrier had been installed all around her, so that even if she somehow came loose, she was still protected. Sturdier than glass but also entirely transparent, it rose like a bubble just over her head. She was sure she wouldn't have even known it was there if Carol hadn't pointed it out to her.

The girl felt far more secure than she had on Cary's back—for which she was thankful as she remembered tumbling toward the ground below.

Carol had greeted her when she woke with a cup of hot apple cider, and had filled the dragon's bowl with some of the same, after the Alfur had finished cleaning out the remnants of the previous evening's stew.

"Please find my Nicky," she had said, her voice quavering ever so slightly with concern.

Elizabeth had hugged her tightly.

Now, Carol bid the dragon and the girl goodbye, waving to them fondly as Dreqnir's wings bore them into the sky above the village. As they rose higher, Elizabeth marveled at how small Carol seemed, this woman with a heart so big that it held a place for all the world's children.

Below, she could see the half-burned ruins of the buildings Dreqnir had scorched with his fire. She could see tiny figures scurrying about and realized that the Alfur were trying to restore them.

"What are those buildings?" the girl asked.

"The factory where all the world's Christmas toys and gifts

are made," Dreqnir said sadly. Elizabeth heard his voice, though not the sound, inside her head—just as she had with Cary. But this time, she could tell it was coming from a definite source: the heart-gem sewn into the lining of her woolen coat.

The dragon continued: "*Even with the Alfur's skills, it may take them time to rebuild them—and to replace the gifts that were lost in the fire. It is my shame and sorrow that I caused such awful destruction.*"

Elizabeth shook her head. "It is not your fault. Tar Kidron is to blame."

"*Ah, but I still did it,*" Dreqnir said. "*This does not ease my guilt.*"

They banked right, toward the east, and Elizabeth heard the sound of the cold wind buffeting the unseen barrier all around her. Inside, the air felt like an early spring day; even as high as they were above the ground, the girl was warmed by Dreqnir's inner fire. Off to the left, a wall of blue-green light glimmered and shimmered from the horizon up into the dark sky.

"What's that?" Elizabeth asked.

"*The Northern Lights. Your people in this region know them as the Revontulet, which means 'Firefox.'*"

"Firefox?"

"*Yes. They tell the story of a wild fox with a burning tail. When she ran through the forest, her fiery tail brushed up against the trees, sending sparks flying up into the night sky. Those sparks danced and shimmered in a wall of gleaming color, which your people call the Aurora Borealis.*"

Elizabeth gasped. "Is that true?"

The dragon chuckled. "*Oh, no. Nor is it true that fallen warriors cross this rainbow bridge into a hall of ceaseless combat and feasting.*"

"That sounds very much like the way our own nations behave," the girl remarked.

"*Indeed. Men love to pretend that the next world is just like this one. It seems to comfort them—even if, in doing so, they continue their suffering.*" He shook his head. "*Humans have such small imaginations! Why not picture a world entirely unlike our own, where wonders not yet known reveal themselves in every moment?*"

"That is the kind of world I would imagine," the girl declared.

"*Which is why, I think, you were fated for this quest. Besides,*" Dreqnir continued, "*they don't want to admit that the lights are really dragon fire, which we use to light our way across the night sky.*"

Elizabeth didn't know whether he was serious about this. But then, by way of demonstration, Dreqnir spewed forth a line of fire that burned brightly out before them, then rained down in colorful sparks on the earth below. The result was very much like the dancing lights away to the north, although Elizabeth still wondered if the story was genuine or merely a legend Dreqnir's own folk had fashioned to explain the lights and their beauty.

"Where do we start looking?" Elizabeth wondered.

"I do not know," the dragon answered. *"Tar Kidron came from Nigel's home, a dark cave city in the cliffs of a secluded fjord. Time acts strangely there, ebbing and flowing like the ocean tide. But I was there, and I know King Nicholas was not there. He would have kept him safely at some distance, in a place so isolated only a few would know of it. Tar Kidron himself did not know where he was taken; if he did, I would have known it, too."*

They flew out across the water, frozen over in many places, and in others dotted by icebergs poking their heads up out of the sea. It seemed they flew for hours before land came again in sight, but the passage of time was difficult to mark without the coming of the sun. Elizabeth slept and woke and slept again, losing track of how long they'd been aloft over the frozen world below. She only knew that she was very tired of sitting in the sleigh seat, as comfortable as it was, by the time a wall of steep cliffs rose up out of the sea before them.

As they drew closer, she saw how jagged they were, like the edge of an unfinished jigsaw puzzle waiting for new pieces. Deep fjords zigzagged in and out of the sea, some rocky and forbidding, others covered with a carpet of green and dotted with lights from homes clustered together in small settlements. Some were fishing villages; others isolated farms. Few of their inhabitants seemed to be out and about, and those who were scurried for cover at the sight of a dragon overhead.

The girl was weary and felt hope draining from her. She so badly wanted to help Carol find King Nicholas, but she had no clue where to look. He could be anywhere, and Dreqnir didn't seem to have any better idea than she did where to begin.

"*My wings are tired,*" the dragon declared, echoing her thoughts. "*My lair is nearby, but it is a secret place. Even though you hold my heart, I must ask a favor: Do you mind covering your eyes as we approach?*"

"Of course not," said the girl, and immediately shut her eyes tightly and covered them with both hands. "I'm ready."

She felt the dragon change course; then he whirled about two or three times in the air, and she lost all sense of direction. Soon, they were descending, Dreqnir flapping his massive wings slowly against the arctic air to slow them, and before long, she felt the dragon touch down as lightly as a sparrow.

Elizabeth removed her hands and opened her eyes and saw that they stood at the apex of an unusually high mountain amidst a range of high mountains. A surreal vista of dark, shadowed peaks, covered in places by frosty white snow, stretched out in all directions. Dreqnir moved forward slowly, deliberately, until he stood at the edge of a precipice. Before them, the mountain fell away into the heart of itself, creating a dark chasm illumined by a glow from deep within.

As massive as Dreqnir was, the abyss before them was far more massive still.

"*Dragehjem,*" Dreqnir said simply. "*Dragon Home.*"

He paused, and the girl could feel tension in his rear haunches as they crouched low to the ground. Then he said, "*Hold on.*"

And jumped.

Chapter Thirteen

Dragon Home

Dreqnir didn't *fly* into the chasm. The dragon's great wings acted like twin parachutes, as he glided downward in tight circles. It might have made Elizabeth dizzy if his descent hadn't been so gradual, like a leaf drifting downward, having been dislodged by a gentle autumn breeze.

The girl had heard of volcanoes, mountains that spewed forth molten fire from deep inside the earth, but this was not one of those. The golden glow below them was pleasantly warm, not unbearable, as she imagined a volcano must be. As they descended farther, she began to see caves carved out into the sides of the great chasm—and some of those caves were occupied.

By dragons.

Some lay sleeping; others stared out at them, curious expressions on their faces. The sight of a little girl sitting in a sleigh on a dragon's back must have seemed peculiar indeed. As she watched, one of the dragons—with shimmering green scales and three horns upon its head—leapt off the edge and descended before them. A few others did the same as they passed, and the girl wondered what might lie ahead.

She soon found out.

When at last they reached the bottom, Dreqnir alighted in the center of a great hall ringed with torches that burned with a magical red-gold hue. The flames didn't dance and flicker so much as they *glowed*, sending their light outward in an aura that extended much farther than typical fire.

"*Dragebrann,*" Dreqnir said. "*There are certain properties that are, shall we say, unique to dragon fire,*" he explained. "*It doesn't just warm and illumine a place, it permeates every corner of it.*"

Dreqnir lowered his entire body to the ground and looked backward, nodding to the girl. In response, she pressed a button on the door of the sleigh, and the invisible barrier that had protected her in flight drew back. She climbed out and down the dragon's tail, the ridges of which acted very much like a staircase. The ground itself, she noticed, was warm beneath her feet.

And, as she looked upward, she noticed they had descended so far that the wide entry to the great chasm was almost lost overhead. Had the moon not been directly above them, she could not have seen it at all.

As she turned her gaze forward again, she noticed that a group of dragons had gathered in a circle all around them. She walked up beside Dreqnir and whispered in one giant ear: "Where are their humans? The ones they are bonded with?"

"*Your kind are not welcome here, even those who are bonded,*" Dreqnir explained silently. "*Be very cautious, and make no sudden movements. They know what Tar Kidron did to me, and they do not trust your presence here—or, most likely, mine.*"

Elizabeth grew very still and looked from one dragon face to another. They all looked curious, but also on their guard. One of them, larger than the rest and larger even, by half again, than the impressively large Dreqnir, stood facing them, brow lowered ominously over two green eyes flecked with gold.

"Why do you bring this *menneskelig* into our presence?" she demanded in a booming voice. "You know such ones are forbidden here."

"The situation is... exceptional," Dreqnir answered, speaking aloud now. "If I may, my queen..."

"You may not, Dreqnir," the large dragon said. "You may be my son and heir, but that does not give you the right to violate our traditions. You yourself are not welcome here, having bound yourself to that... that monster. Did he send you here? Is this *menneskelig* his agent? Or perhaps it is the monster himself in disguise! I have heard he has a talent for such trickery, just like his master, Lord Nigel."

"It is not, mother. I am no longer bonded to Tar Kidron. I am bonded now to this one." He nodded toward Elizabeth.

"Tar Kidron released his bond to you? Willingly? I do not believe it! He has told you to say this, in order to deceive us."

"He did not, Mother," Dreqnir said. And then silently, to Elizabeth: "*Show her my heart-gem.*"

Slowly, Elizabeth reached inside her coat and loosened the leather cord that held in place a flap to an inner pouch. That pouch contained Dreqnir's ruby heart-gem. She saw the dragons' muscles tense as they watched her, perhaps expecting her to withdraw some weapon. Several of them gasped when she produced the stone instead.

"That proves nothing," the Dragon Queen scoffed. "The monster is a master of deceit. He could have forced you to bring him here, while taking the form of this small *menneskelig* to trick us."

The green-scaled, three-horned dragon who had first seen them on their arrival stepped forward, and Dreqnir released an audible sigh. He turned to Elizabeth:

"Dreqalan will not harm you," he said. "But I fear I must ask you to go with him. It is the only way to persuade my mother that you are who I say you are."

Elizabeth nodded and followed the one called Dreqalan, who took her to a small recess in the rock wall of the cavern. Once she was inside, he left her there, closing her in with a precisely hewn stone door. A torch lit with dragon fire burned silently in one corner, and she noticed something else about it: It did not give off any smoke, nor did it appear to need air to fuel its flame. Still, it warmed her, and made her feel a little less anxious about being left all alone inside such a place, which admitted neither sight nor sound from beyond its walls.

Thankfully, she was only there a few moments before Dreqalan returned and escorted her out.

When she returned to the dragon circle, she noticed at once that the tensions seemed to have eased, and the expression on the Dragon Queen's face was far more placid than it had been earlier.

"You are welcome here," she said, addressing Elizabeth, though it was not exactly the sort of warm and open welcome she had received from Carol in her village. "I can see that you have questions. I will do my best to answer those that I deem prudent to address."

Dreqnir scowled at this, clearly annoyed at his mother's overly formal demeanor.

She either did not notice or ignored it, and

continued: "We dragons have a certain oath that is inviolable. Once it is sworn, we know the oath-giver speaks the truth. For obvious reasons, we do not permit the *menneskelig*—or anyone else—to know it, which is why you were secluded these past few moments. The oath is more sacred to us even than the bond you share with my son." She nodded toward Dreqnir. "Were he to break it, the heart-gem would shatter, and he would die."

The girl's eyes widened as she heard this, but she said nothing.

"Because Dreqnir has taken this oath—and survived—we know that you are not Tar Kidron, nor are you one of his agents."

Elizabeth breathed a sigh of relief.

"Nevertheless, Dreqnir has violated our traditions by bringing you here, even considering the purpose of your journey. He has told us of your quest to find King Nicholas, and he has always been a friend to our kind. Nothing would give us greater pleasure than to help you. Sadly, though, none of us has seen him. I fear we cannot help you."

Elizabeth's face was downcast.

But just then, a stout blue dragon with smaller wings and a ridged crest like a rooster's comb atop her head stepped forward. "Beggin' your pardon, Majesty," she said, "but perhaps, in fact, we can."

All of them turned toward her.

"Karanadreq," the queen said, by way of introduction. "She is our treasurer."

"Treasurer?" the girl said, speaking aloud despite herself.

The queen laughed. "Of course," she said. "Have you ever heard of a dragon's lair without a treasure?"

Elizabeth had to admit she hadn't, although she hadn't heard of one *with* a treasure, either, since she had heard very little about dragons at all.

The queen turned to Karanadreq. "What news, then?"

Karanadreq bowed awkwardly. "If it please Your Majesty, it concerns the inventory."

The Dragon Queen frowned. "The inventory? How does this relate to the matter at hand? Is something missing?"

"Not exactly, Your Majesty."

"What, then?" The queen was clearly growing impatient. "Out with it."

"Well, Your Majesty, nothing is *missing*. It's the opposite, actually: Something has appeared that didn't used to be there."

The queen's frown deepened. "Are you sure it is not just some new addition that has been brought in by one of our number?"

"Absolutely." Karanadreq's tone was firm and decisive. "I *always* check *everything* in when it arrives.

These items were not brought to us by any of our number."

"Is it possible that they were there all along? Perhaps misfiled or overlooked?"

Now it was Karanadreq's turn to grow impatient. She clearly took great pride in her oversight of the treasure, and she was upset that her diligence and competence were being questioned. "They were *not* misfiled or overlooked, Majesty," she said. "They simply... appeared."

"Well, then," the queen said, trying to check her own impatience, "what exactly *are* these items?"

Karanadreq was obviously prepared for this question, because she immediately produced two items. One was a papyrus scroll, and the other a small... something... set in gold. She brought them both forward and handed them to the queen.

"A compass," the queen said simply, then turned her attention to the scroll and unrolled it. "A map."

A small orange dragon, who had been standing silently in a far corner through all this, watching from a distance, let out a sudden yelp.

The queen looked over at him. "Do you know something about this, Dreqfal?"

The orange dragon ambled forward, almost like a penguin. He was only about half the size of Dreqnir, and seemed far older: Some of his scales were chipped, and his eyes were deep-set and soft gray. "I believe so, Your Majesty. If you will indulge me."

The queen nodded once sharply.

"If I am not mistaken, these appear to be two of the legendary Talismans of Time: the Compass of the Seventh Kingdom and the Map of Gildersleeve."

The Dragon Queen shook her head. "I have not heard of them," she said. "Are they significant?"

"Indeed," said Dreqfal. "They are said to work together, at least according to the legends I have heard. The compass points the way toward the heart's desire of the one who holds it, and the map displays the pathway to arrive there."

Elizabeth blinked once and felt her heart quicken. Could this be a way to find King Nicholas?

Dreqnir was obviously thinking the same thing. "Mother," he said. "I believe we can put these to good use."

The queen nodded slowly. She seemed to be considering. "You know it is our custom not to part with anything in our treasury," she said slowly.

"Anything in our *inventory*," Karanadreq put in. "That is the language in our bylaws."

"And you said yourself these items were *not* in the inventory," Dreqnir replied.

"Indeed," said Karanadreq.

The Dragon Queen seemed to be considering, then

finally shook her head. "I'm sorry, my son, but I cannot abide it."

Elizabeth's shoulders slumped, but Dreqnir's ears perked up, and he raised his head to its full height.

The girl felt a sudden twinge of anxiety, and wondered where it came from. Then she realized it hadn't come from her own breast, but from the heart-gem she wore in the lining of her coat. Dreqnir was worried. More than worried, he was alarmed. She would have expected him to be disappointed at his mother's words, but not that he would be so disquieted. But before the girl could question his reaction, it changed: Alarm became anger, and anger became fury.

The next few words rolled off his long tongue methodically, one at a time: "What did you say, *Mother*?"

The Dragon Queen blinked once, then again, more slowly, but said nothing.

And in that moment, Dreqnir launched himself at her in a rage. As Elizabeth watched in amazement, the Dragon Queen shifted form and collapsed back in on herself, becoming much smaller and much... different. Her wings faded and vanished, her scales disappeared, and her color darkened from orange-gold to black. That was the color of a robe she now wore—except that "she" was now a *he*: a tall and slender man with a long, gray beard that flowed down almost to his waist. In the same instant that Dreqnir flew at him, he raised a crooked wooden staff out in front of him, and the massive dragon seemed to slow down. Dreqnir looked almost suspended in midair as the black-cloaked figure stepped aside and out of his path. Then he pivoted, thrust his staff high into the air, and vanished in a white-hot flash as bright and sudden as lightning crashing down from heaven.

As soon as he was gone, Dreqnir came crashing to the ground, claws slashing and fire flaring from his nostrils. He landed where the robed man had stood a moment earlier, then rose up on his hind legs and let out an ear-splitting roar.

The other dragons were all scrambling around, some of them flying frantically overhead, others scurrying for cover.

The girl stood there and watched it all, unsure how to take any of it.

What had happened?

"*My mother is gone!*" came the answer, unspoken, in Dreqnir's mind-voice. "*The Time Master kidnapped her and took her place!*" The cave floor shook as he dropped back down on all fours.

"The Time Master?"

"Lord Nigel," he nearly shouted. "Or 'Father Time,' as he fashions himself." He calmed his voice somewhat as he continued: "He has the ability, not only to warp time, but to reshape appearances to his own ends. Clearly, he did this, and somehow managed to subdue my mother and take her place upon the throne."

"But how did you know it was him?" the girl asked.

"Oh, he was very convincing," Dreqnir admitted. "There was nothing in her—or *his*—appearance that seemed unusual. It wasn't anything he did. It was something he said: 'I cannot abide it.' I've never heard my mother say anything like that; she may stand on formality, but she is never condescending. On the other hand, I *have* heard Tar Kidron use that very phrase many times. I always thought it strange that he would speak in such a way, as though he were a member of some noble house, and he explained to me that it was something he'd heard from Lord Nigel."

His voice rose again: "Now Lord Nigel has King Nicholas, he has my mother, and he has the talismans, as well!"

"Not exactly."

Dreqnir and Elizabeth both turned toward the source of the voice. Karanadreq stood there, holding the map in one hand and the compass in the other.

"How...?" Dreqnir's voice trailed off.

"Thank you for distracting him," Karanadreq replied calmly. "While his attention was on you, I was able to... relieve him of the items." She paused, and then said, "I take my responsibility to curate our inventory very seriously."

Dreqnir walked over to Karanadreq, opened his

wings, and wrapped her up in them so completely that she all but disappeared. “Thank you, Karana,” he said warmly. “Thanks to you, we have the means to find my mother. And King Nicholas.”

Chapter Fourteen

Bull-headed

Once again, the boy found himself alone. Likho had demanded that Django get out of his sight and had banished him from the forest. The young Romani had left without protest, hurrying back the way they had come and disappearing into the darkness. Alex wondered idly whether Django would be able to find his way out of the underground maze on his own; he hoped Likho would be lenient enough to let Xander accompany him, although he had to admit the tree-man didn't seem particularly merciful.

Alex didn't have time to worry about Django now, though. He sat on a moss-covered stump in the middle of the Black Forest—made blacker than its name by the perpetual night—with no idea where to turn. He had placed all his hope in the compass and the map, and both of these were now lost to him, presumably forever. He tried to console himself with the knowledge that someone else, somewhere else, might be saved by them. But he did not know the little girl Likho had spoken of, so he couldn't even picture her in his mind's eye. She was just a nameless, faceless someone who would be able to find her way home because of him. But he felt farther from home than ever, and more alone than he had felt in his entire life.

To make matters worse, Likho had promised to direct him to the next talisman in his quest—the Flute of Pan's Third Daughter—but had neglected to do so, and the boy had forgotten to remind him.

Now he had nowhere to go and no one to help him.

He leaned over, put his head in his hands, and cried, his body shaking silently with each new sob as tears poured down from his eyes.

His sorrow was such that he barely noticed a rustling of leaves off to his left, or the woman who emerged from the underbrush just a few steps away.

At last, he raised his head, and gasped in surprise, hurriedly wiping his tears away.

Alamina looked somehow taller than she had before, perhaps because the boy himself felt so very small. Once she knew that he had seen her, she nodded once and smiled slightly in greeting.

Alex scrambled to his feet. "Are you looking for Django?" he asked.

She shook her head and laughed. "Oh, no. He can find his way home," she said, in a tone that sounded unconcerned, disappointed and a bit annoyed all at once. "I have contacted Likho, and he has promised no harm will befall my child." She paused briefly. "Though I do worry about Django's lack of judgment. I *did* tell him I would be watching the two of you!"

She sighed. "He is still young and in need of instruction. Fortunately, that is something we can provide."

Alex wondered who she meant by "we," but said nothing, she continued: "I did not come here to find him. I came here to find you."

Then it dawned on Alex: She wanted the compass back.

"I don't have the talisman," he said in a worried voice.

Alamina laughed again. "I know," she said. "Remember, I was watching you!"

"Oh."

"I don't want the compass back," she assured him. "It was freely given and freely accepted. It was therefore yours to do with as you saw fit. If it helps at all, I approve of your decision more than you could possibly know."

Alex relaxed a little.

"I am only here," she said, "because you looked so very alone. I thought you might appreciate some company."

The boy's face brightened. "Are you coming with me?"

But Alamina shook her head. "No, child. I have children who need me, and many others, as well. I cannot leave them unattended. They would have no idea what to do with themselves if I weren't there to take care of them." Her tone was not haughty, but straightforward. "Besides, I want to be there when Django returns.

"No," she continued, "I will not be coming with you. But I brought you two companions to keep you from being so lonely—and, perhaps, to help you in your quest."

As if on cue, a flash of gray fur came zipping out of the underbrush, followed closely by a loudly panting, droopy-faced dog. The gray blur ran rings around the bloodhound, seemingly taunting him with its speed. It moved so quickly, it took a moment for Alex to realize exactly what it was: a large gray-and-black tabby cat. But this was no ordinary feline. It had more than one tail—although it was moving so fast that he couldn't tell exactly *how many* tails there were. The tabby dashed about in circles and figure-eights, occasionally leaping over her pursuer, until the bloodhound grew so dizzy he fell down in a heap on the ground. There he lay, panting and whining softly, as the cat leapt into Alamina's arms.

She began petting the tabby softly.

"This," she said, "is Isis." Then, nodding toward the boy, she said, "Isis, this is Alexander."

The cat opened her mouth and yawned, then began licking her left paw.

"Pardon her rudeness," Alamina said. "She is, after all, a cat. She is named after a goddess because she thinks she is one."

Isis hissed and began waving her multiple tails about indignantly. "That is not nice," she said. "I am who I am, and I like myself that way."

The fact that Isis spoke did not surprise the boy, who had so far encountered a scarecrow, a crow, and a tree-man, all of whom could talk. What did surprise him was how many tails Isis had: He could count them now and saw that there were nine of them, all waving about in a distracting but somehow hypnotic manner.

"Isis is a cat of nine tails," Alamina explained.

"She thinks she's special." The low, deep voice belonged to the dog, whose tone was decidedly sardonic.

"And this," Alamina said, "is Ruffus. He is a bloodhound."

At least Alex knew what a bloodhound was.

"Isis and Ruffus each have a special talent that you may find helpful in your journey. Ruffus is no ordinary bloodhound. He can recognize any scent, whether he has encountered it before or not."

Isis meowed. "He thinks he's special," she purred in mock admiration, her voice so syrupy that it might have come from a maple tree.

Alamina ignored her.

"Isis, on the other hand, has a talent for misdirection."

"So, they're kind of opposites," the boy said.

Alamina chuckled. "I suppose so. And in more ways than one. But Isis is every bit as helpful as Ruffus: Her tails are not only many, but they are magical. She can use them to distract and mesmerize an adversary at a crucial moment."

Isis began purring, and Alamina ran her fingers through the feline's soft, warm fur. The woman cupped her hand to one side of her mouth conspiratorially. "She likes her *ego* stroked, too."

She winked.

Alex couldn't help but thinking that Django would be dismayed to find Isis gone when he returned, just as he had been distressed that his mother had parted with the compass. Isis, he imagined, could be a powerful ally to anyone intent on… acquiring things.

"Yeah. Special," Ruffus said.

Isis purred all more loudly.

"Can they get along?" Alex wondered aloud.

"We don't get along very well with children who speak in our presence as though we weren't here," Isis quipped.

"Sorry," said the boy.

"Apology accepted," said the cat.

"I can get along with her, as long as she stops trying to throw me off the scent," Ruffus said, then glared at Isis. "You can't, you know."

"We'll see about that," Isis tittered.

Ruffus howled, then stopped suddenly, stuck his nose in the air, and began sniffing excitedly. Then, just as suddenly, he stopped, turned toward a particularly dense section of woodland, and bounded away.

"You'd better follow him," Alamina said. "When he latches onto a scent, he forgets about everything else."

Isis yawned, unconcerned. "Not that he knew all that much to begin with," she said, then sighed. "But Mina's right. We'd better go after him." The cat hopped up on the boy's shoulder. "You're my ride."

"Thank you!" Alex said to Alamina, who merely nodded in the direction Ruffus had gone.

And the boy followed, leaving her behind.

"He's so impetuous," Isis complained, trying to groom herself as the boy trotted along. "No need to jostle me so," she added. "I'm a delicate creature."

The term "high maintenance" jumped into the boy's thoughts. He didn't know where he'd heard it, but he was certain it applied to Isis.

Fortunately, bloodhounds are meticulous about following their scent and not particularly fast, so they were able to catch up to Ruffus without too much trouble. He was standing on the bank of a river, staring across into the darkness. Alex thought it must be the river that Django had mentioned, but it was like none he had ever imagined. Its waters were glassy black, even where they should have foamed up as they ran over rocks. It was so wide he couldn't see the far side of it: No wonder Django had despaired of getting across.

Nonetheless, Ruffus was pointing his nose directly at it, indicating that the scent ended there.

"You expect me to get my fur wet in *that*?" said Isis, incredulous.

"I'll keep you on my shoulders," Alex said, trying to reassure her.

"Until you go under," she scoffed.

"I could try to carry you," Ruffus suggested.

Isis sighed a catty sigh. "I'll take my chances with the human."

Alex took a step into the water. It didn't seem too swift here, so he took another step and, feeling more confident, began to wade into the river. Ruffus, being a typical dog, bounded directly in—and was swept so far into the darkness that Alex immediately lost sight of him.

"What—? he started to say, but before he could get anything else out of his mouth, a strong current grabbed him, catapulting him head-over-heels downstream. It was almost like being hit by an ocean wave. It thrust him like a human pinwheel in a wild whirl that forced him underwater, pulled him out again, and thrust him down once more in a dizzying spin. Water invaded his windpipe; he coughed and spat it out. Isis's claws dug deep into his shoulder and then were gone as she was ripped away from him in the rapids. Alex had always thought of himself as a capable swimmer, but this current was too ferocious even for him. He knew better than to panic, but began to panic anyway, arms and legs flailing as he was carried inexorably forward, toward he knew not what.

All of a sudden, something hit him in the chest: a branch that had fallen across the watercourse, knocking what was left of his breath out of him.

Instinctively, he grabbed it and clung on in desperation, pulling himself up out of the water and climbing across it, hand over hand, like a jungle gym, with his feet still dangling down into the river.

Somehow, amazingly, he managed to reach the shore, where he collapsed in a heap near a mossy rock.

"Fancy meeting you here."

Alex tried to catch his breath as he turned his head toward the sound of the voice. It was Isis. The feline had apparently grabbed hold of the branch and made her way to shore, as well. Her fur was drenched and clung to her body, making her appear about half the size she had seemed when she'd been dry. Her nine tails whipped and waved in deep annoyance.

"Where's Ruffus?" said Alex.

Just then, the bloodhound bounded up out of the river, shaking himself emphatically the way dogs do when they get wet.

"I've never been in a river like that," he said. "It was a bit unnerving."

"Water in general is 'unnerving,' as you put it," Isis sneered, and she started grooming herself.

Ruffus ignored her. "I smell something."

"It's probably your body odor," said Isis.

The bloodhound continued to ignore her, and trotted over to a nearby tree. He zigged and zagged a bit on his way, trying to regain his equilibrium after being tossed and turned unmercifully in the current. But despite this, he knew exactly where he was going. He stopped at the trunk of the tree, which was particularly large, and stood at the edge of a dense thicket. There, he put his nose to the ground and began circling the tree intently, first one direction, then back the other way.

"What is it, boy?" Alex asked.

Ruffus raised his head momentarily. "Don't call me boy," he said, voice full of disdain. Isis wasn't the only one who was high maintenance.

"Sorry," the boy said.

"To answer your question, I'm not sure what it is," the bloodhound replied. "But I do know it's *something*."

That much, the boy thought, was obvious. The question was whether it was something important.

Ruffus resumed his task, continuing in circles around the tree, which was wide enough that he disappeared entirely when he went around the other side, only to re-emerge a moment later. The tree itself looked dead, having been struck by lightning at some point and hollowed out, either by the thunderbolt itself or by insects. Alex hoped it was the former. He didn't like bugs much.

He followed Ruffus around the trunk.

"There's a hole here in the side of it," he said. "Maybe whatever you're smelling is inside."

"A logical conclusion," said Isis. "Plain as the nose on his face." She nodded toward the bloodhound. "But *he* would rather chase his tail."

Ruffus snorted. "Just making sure," he said scornfully. "Someone *might* be trying to throw us off the scent."

The cat's eyes widened as if to say, "Who? Me?" Then she decided to ignore him and resumed her grooming.

Alex stepped through the mossy hole and into the tree. Ruffus followed, then moved back in front of him and started sniffing again. The tree seemed somehow larger on the inside than it had on the outside. *Much* larger, as a matter of fact. It no longer seemed so much a tree as a grand hall, with banners hung on walls illumined by flickering torches. This struck the boy as rather dangerous, considering trees are made of wood. Perhaps, he thought to himself, the tree hadn't been hit by lightning at all, but burned by one of these torches.

Isis paused her grooming and looked up momentarily. She seemed to know what he'd been thinking. "The walls are coated with a resin that keeps them from catching fire," she observed.

"Yes," confirmed Ruffus. "I can smell it."

"Oh, you're so talented!" Isis mocked. "Even *I* can smell it."

"Cats," the bloodhound muttered, and put his nose back on the floor again.

That was another thing about this place: It had a floor. The bare earth they might have expected to find inside a tree had been replaced by a solid floor, inlaid with an intricate mosaic in shades of blue and tan and silver. Blue dolphins swam around the sides of it, which were ringed by near-circular swirls that the boy decided must be stylized waves. It was odd, he thought, that sea creatures would be depicted here in the midst of a forest, so far from the ocean. But then he remembered that distance seemed to have become meaningless since he entered the corn maze. Was he still *in* the corn maze? He didn't *appear* to be, but something told him he was. Things on the inside didn't seem to be what they were on the outside. Take this tree, for instance. It was like a TV show he'd seen once, with a police call box that was actually a machine made for traveling through space and time. It was much bigger on the inside, too...

Ruffus looked up. "What's that smell?" he said.

Isis meowed. "Aren't *you* supposed to tell *us* that?"

The bloodhound ignored her and went back to sniffing.

Alex turned his attention back to the mosaic floor. At the center of it was something even stranger than the dolphins: A large bull, head lowered as if it were charging, stood between two slender human figures. One seemed to be holding its horns—or perhaps was being gored by the beast; the second stood behind it, arms outstretched toward a third figure, which looked like it was doing a summersault over the back of the creature.

Isis was looking down at it too, from her perch on Alex's shoulder. "Humans have such poor judgment," she said calmly.

Ruffus looked up again from his sniffing. His nose had been pressed to the floor, near the bull's hindquarters.

"I smell bull," he declared.

"I'm not surprised," Isis said drily.

Ruffus shook his head, as if trying to dislodge the scent from his nostrils. "I have a bad feeling about this."

"Scaredy dog," Isis mocked.

"I don't think so," the boy said. "I'm scared, too. Something doesn't feel right."

"I think we should go back the way we came," Ruffus said, his tone suddenly anxious.

"Oh, whatever," said Isis, but she had stopped grooming herself, and her lazy-sleepy eyes were all the way open.

Alex turned around. "Yes," he said. "Let's go."

But as he looked back in the direction from which they'd come, the boy saw only darkness. The torchlight stopped abruptly at a certain place, beyond which there seemed to be a solid wall of black. There was no sign of the door through which they'd entered, which should have been just a few steps behind them.

"Uh oh," said Isis.

Alex heard the bloodhound gulp as he stepped back toward the blackness.

"The scent... just stops," he said.

"Which scent?" the boy asked.

"All of them."

Alex stepped forward, past Ruffus—and bumped

headlong into a solid wall.

"Ouch!"

The wall should have been visible in the torchlight, but somehow it wasn't. It didn't reflect any of the light that should have bounced off of it, but instead seemed to be absorbing it.

Alex put both hands up and started feeling his way along it. It was solid, with no breaks, in both directions. Where was the door?

"You can't get out. Believe me, I've tried."

The voice didn't belong to Isis or Ruffus.

Alex turned back to see an odd-looking figure standing before them—and towering over them. Dressed in a blue suit with a purple tie, the giant looked like any other businessman ready for a day at the office. Except for one thing: He had the head of a bull, not unlike the one depicted in the mosaic. Two long horns twisted outward from his head, making him look not unlike a demon.

"Welcome to the Minute-Hour Hotel," he said. "You can check out anytime you like, but I'm afraid you can never leave."

"Who are you?" said Alex, forgetting his manners.

"My name is Asterion," said the bull-headed man. "I'm afraid you've stumbled into my prison. At least I have some company now—for the time being."

"What do you mean, 'for the time being'?" the boy

asked.

"He means that, eventually, he'll get hungry and he'll have to eat us," Isis said. "That's how it works."

The bull-headed man nodded slowly. "I'm afraid she's right," he allowed. "It's nothing personal. I have to eat."

Alex was suddenly worried. "Why don't you eat berries or something," he suggested, forgetting that few such edible options existed in Likho's realm. "Find something in the forest. Besides, I didn't think bulls ate meat. Shouldn't you be eating grass or something?"

Asterion laughed sardonically. "I'm not a bull. I'm a man. I just happen to have a bull's head," he said, as if that explained everything. "I prefer bacon to berries, but even if I liked them, they wouldn't do me any good. In case you haven't noticed, I can't get to the forest. I'm stuck in here. Now, so are you."

He stepped back from them toward a kettle on a woodstove. Oddly, there didn't seem to be any wood in the stove, but a fire burned there, nonetheless. No smoke rose from it, and Alex noticed for the first time that the torches didn't give off any smoke, either. "The least I can do is offer you a hot beverage to comfort you," he said. "Do you fancy some tea?"

"Why a hot beverage?" asked Alex.

Asterion shrugged. "It's the cultural convention."

"All right," said Alex.

"Good," said Asterion. "The ginger and honey will season you for when it comes time for me to eat you."

"I think I'll pass on the tea," said Isis.

"Me too," said Ruffus.

The bull-man shrugged. "Suit yourself. I don't eat dog or cat meat, anyway." He gestured toward a large, circular table, where he sat and bade Alex join him.

Ruffus resumed sniffing around the edges of the room.

"Go ahead," said Asterion. "You won't find a way out. My father instructed his friend Daedalus to make this place impregnable, and Daedalus is the finest craftsman in all of Crete. He even made wings for his son to fly, but that didn't turn out as well as he had hoped."

"Crete?" said Alex.

"Yes, the island. In the Middle-Earth Sea. The height of civilization—except when it comes to the whole vengeance thing. Not very civilized, that."

The answer only confused Alex all the more. He had started out in Iowa, had been transported somehow to Germany's Black Forest, and now he was on an island in Middle Earth?

"Are there hobbits here?" he asked, chagrined.

"Not *that* Middle Earth," said Isis. "He means the Mediterranean Sea. 'Mediterranean' means 'Middle Earth.'"

"Oh," said Alex.

That explained the name, but it didn't explain how he'd gotten here. He decided it wouldn't do him any good to pursue that line of inquiry. He didn't want to feel even more bewildered than he already was. Besides, he had other questions.

"I don't mean to be rude," he said. "But why do you have a bull's head?"

"Haven't you ever heard the story of the Minute-Hour?" said Asterion.

Isis meowed. "I always thought it was pronounced 'Minotaur.'" She never missed an opportunity to look superior, but this time, the effort backfired.

"Translations tend to get garbled with the passage of centuries," Asterion explained.

Isis, who didn't like to be corrected about correcting someone else, set about feverishly grooming the spot right under her chin that was most difficult to reach.

Alex *had* heard the story, now that he thought about it. But it had taken place uncounted centuries ago, in a time of legend. How was it that the bull-man was still alive? It wasn't just space, but time that operated strangely in this place.

"To answer your question about my... appearance," Asterion said, "I was born like this. My father, the king, was ashamed of me, so he had me imprisoned at the center of this labyrinth so no one would ever see my face. He cursed my poor mother and blamed her for my deformity. He disowned me and said I was no son of his, but the child of a beast. He blamed Poseidon, the god of the sea, because he—my father—had failed to sacrifice a bull to him. So he said I had become the bull that he must sacrifice."

"How primitive," said Isis.

Alex ignored her. He had heard something that made him set down his teacup and listen more carefully. "What did you mean," he asked, "when you said that you are at the center of a labyrinth? Like a maze?"

"A maze and a labyrinth are slightly different," Isis observed.

"Close enough," said Ruffus.

Alex remembered what the scarecrow had said at the beginning of his journey. The kobold had said it, too: He would have to reach the center of the maze before he could find his way home. If *this* was the center of the maze, he was halfway to his destination. All he had to do now was find a way out.

"Daedalus sealed me in and left me here. Every now and then, my father sends children my way so I can eat them."

"Lovely," said Isis.

"Wait," said Alex. "Did Daedalus come in here with you, *then* leave?"

"Yes."

"Then there must be a way out! How did he escape?"

The Minute-Hour shrugged. "Who knows?" he said. "Daedalus might be able to tell you, if you could find him. But the last anyone saw of him, he had gone into hiding, mourning for his son, Icarus. Those wings Daedalus created for him? They worked *too* well. Icarus ended up flying too close to the sun and... well, you've heard the expression 'it's better to burn out than fade away'? That isn't always true."

"That's too bad," said Alex, but he was more concerned about himself at this point. "If Daedalus found a way out of this maze... er... labyrinth, there must be a way out for *us* to find, too!"

"Stands to reason," said Isis.

But Ruffus huffed, "If there is, I can't find it. And I can find *anything*."

"Just like a dog. Such blind conceit."

"Look who's talking."

"Please!" said the boy. "Stop arguing! If you keep going, I'll be glad to have Asterion eat me, just so I can stop listening to the two of you bicker!"

Cat and dog both fell silent, but neither one apologized. Instead, they set about glaring at one another.

"More tea?" asked the Minute-Hour.

Alex waved his hand and stood; walking over to where Ruffus was, he started exploring again along the wall.

"Suit yourself." Asterion poured himself another cup and sat back, sipping away as he watched them.

When he had finished, he reached into the top drawer of a chest beside him and pulled out a golden flute.

He began playing it, and the music filled the room.

Chapter Fifteen

Up in the Air

The compass was going crazy. Its needle spun in circles clockwise, then back in the opposite direction. It was either broken or indecisive. Or both.

Without the compass, the map was of no help.

"If we turn west, it says to go north. If we turn north, it tells us to go east!" the girl said. "Where on earth could they be?"

"What if they are not on earth?" said Dreqnir.

"What do you mean?"

"Try pointing the compass on its side."

Elizabeth was unclear about what this might accomplish, but she did as the dragon suggested, nonetheless. It couldn't hurt.

The circular compass, with its rounded edge, wouldn't stay upright when placed on its side, so Elizabeth had to keep hold of it. As she did, she watched—and marveled as the needle settled into place and held steady.

It was pointing straight up, at the sky.

"How convenient," Dreqnir said, a hint of self-satisfaction apparent in his tone. He extended his wings. "Climb aboard!"

He lowered his body to the ground, allowing Elizabeth to climb up onto his back and into the specially fitted sleigh the Alfur had crafted for her. When she was securely fastened in, Dreqnir crouched on his hind legs and sprang upward like an arrow, heading toward the opening overhead faster than the girl had ever seen him fly. It was clear he was worried about his mother. She could feel the heart-gem pumping against her chest, fear about the queen's fate mixed with anger toward Nigel, pulsating out from it in nearly equal measure.

Within moments, they were clear of the *Dragehjem* cavern, soaring upward into the black-night sky that covered all the land. The girl could feel the heaviness of it upon her; she missed the sun on her face and the blue sky overhead. Like most things humans take for granted, she didn't realize *how much* she missed it until it was taken from her. The Northern Lights off to her left offered some small comfort, and she wondered whether dragons like Dreqnir were breathing their fiery breath to help guide their way.

As Dreqnir leveled the course of his flight, Elizabeth glanced down at the compass and saw that it was pointing off slightly to her right. She relayed this information to Dreqnir, who adjusted his path accordingly. He rose slightly as he flew parallel to the Scandes, the mountain range that formed the spine of the Scandinavian Peninsula in Norway. Glaciers stretched out beneath them, like white rivers literally frozen in time. She saw the names of individual peaks appear magically on the Map of Gildersleeve as they grew closer: names like Galdhøpiggen and Glittertind, Surtningssue and Skarstind. She could not even pronounce some of them; the letters in fine calligraphy appeared to write themselves across the parchment as they approached, then faded gradually as they moved away from the landmarks below. She had never seen anything like it.

Each time the compass needle moved, she alerted Dreqnir, who changed his course to match it. Beneath them, deep gorges and canyons cut between the peaks of snowcapped mountains. The needle started quivering, as if in excitement, just before Dreqnir suddenly came to a stop and began circling in midair.

"What's wrong?" asked Elizabeth.

"*There's a barrier here,*" Dreqnir said through the heartstone. "I can feel the energy of it just ahead."

"I can't see anything."

"It's invisible, held in place by magic. I've come across it before, and I always simply went around it. It never occurred to me to ask why it was here. I always assumed some wizard valued his privacy—the way we dragons do."

"Is there a barrier around your Dragon Home?"

"*Yes*," said Dreqnir. "*You were only able to pass it because I accompanied you. I don't know how Nigel was able to thwart its magic, much less kidnap my mother undetected. But his magic is powerful, and he is not only a Time Wielder, but a Shape Changer—a master of disguise, as you have seen.*"

"Do you think he's here, beyond this barrier?"

"*Is that where the compass is pointing?*" Dreqnir asked.

"Yes."

"*Then he is here. It will be a challenge to surprise him before he can disappear again—if, that is, we even find a way through his barrier.*"

"What if we just tried to fly through it?"

Dreqnir looked back over his shoulder at her, as though he thought she was crazy.

"The longer we stay here, the more the needle on the compass jumps around. It's as if it *wants* us to keep going."

Dreqnir raised an eye ridge—where the brow would have been on a human—intrigued. "*Perhaps there is magic in the compass that will take us through*," he mused. "*I suppose it is worth a try. But if we bump headlong into the barrier, I'll put the blame on you!"*

Elizabeth laughed a nervous laugh. "Go slow then," she said.

Dreqnir eased forward, flapping his wings down, then forward to slow his progress. Elizabeth could tell from the feeling in his heart-gem that he was nervous. She could also feel the energy of the barrier now, buzzing and humming a low, steady buzz-hum that was more a feeling than a sound, burrowing its way beneath her skin. It itched and tickled her all over, and she shivered involuntarily. The feeling grew stronger as they moved forward, and the girl imagined the dragon must feel it all the more outside the invisible bubble that shielded her.

A few moments later, the buzz-hum seemed to almost envelop her. Then she felt a sudden POP! like a rubber band snapping, propelling them forward with a jerk.

"*We're through!*" said Dreqnir, gliding down low and shadowing the peaks beneath him. "*We need to maintain the element of surprise.*"

"Do we know what we're looking for?" the girl asked.

"*I have no idea.*"

But just as Dreqnir was communicating this, they rounded a jagged outcropping and came in sight of a floating city. Dozens of colorful balloons, in reds and tans, yellows and oranges, hovered just below the mountain peaks, anchored to the valley below by sturdy ropes. The balloons themselves were so massive they held up wooden structures the size of houses or even larger. They were connected by gangways and rope ladders, making them look very much like galleons and schooners of the air.

Dreqnir landed on the outcropping and pulled back, just out of sight, then peered around the corner of the mountain.

"I've heard of this place," he said, *"but have never seen it. I doubt many people have."*

"What is it?" the girl asked.

"A moving marketplace called Airborne. It's run by illicit traders, who move from place to place and ply their wares among the less savory elements: bandits, slavers, and opportunists. What does the compass say? Does it still point in that direction?"

"It does. What does it mean?"

"Either Nigel is trying to mask his presence by taking refuge here, or he has some sort of business. I only hope he does not seek to sell my mother into slavery and force a bond upon her."

Elizabeth gasped. "Can he do that?"

"I do not know. But perhaps we can find her. If you adjust your spectacles to magnify things at a distance, perhaps you can tell where they may be holding her."

The spectacles! Elizabeth had almost forgotten she was wearing them. She felt a pang of guilt: If she'd even suspected the so-called dragon queen was really Lord Nigel in disguise, she would have adjusted them to their most helpful setting: "to see things as they truly are." But she'd had no reason to suspect someone might have infiltrated the Dragon Home. Lord Nigel had even fooled Dreqnir for some time. How could she possibly have known?

"*You could not have,*" said Dreqnir, reading her thoughts. "*Do not blame yourself.*"

The girl adjusted the glasses to their magnifying setting, allowing her to see things far more closely than before. She saw men walking between the balloon ships, carrying barrels and crates across narrow gangways, and she wondered how they seemed so sure of their steps so far above the ground. She saw a man and a woman appearing to argue over a purple cloak, the man pulling on one end and the woman on the other, until the man lost his grip and fell over backward. He rose, shaking his fist at the woman, and stomped away. She saw a man in a turban on a pedestal, standing next to a man in shackles and tattered clothes. A group of men and a few women stood in front of the podium; one would occasionally raise a hand, then another would do the same. Finally, one of them stepped forward and took custody of the shackled man, shoving him roughly forward in front of them.

She saw no sign of the Dragon Queen or King

Nicholas.

Disappointed, Elizabeth decided to adjust the spectacles again, this time to the setting she had failed to use before: She wanted to see things as they truly were. Moving the lenses up and down until she found the right combination, and the resulting picture was very different than what she'd seen before. Each small figure aboard the floating ships was surrounded by a faint glow or aura, all in varied colors. Many of them were dark gray or even black, and this, she surmised, meant they were somehow of questionable character. Considering what Dreqnir had said about the place being a haven for thieves and unscrupulous merchants, this hardly seemed surprising. A few auras were red; a few were yellow, and one or two were blue. The red seemed fiery, and she could tell by the body language of those with such auras that they were angry. The yellow fluctuated, and individuals with this color seemed to have a spring in their step: They were happy. The blue auras surrounded people who seemed to be standing or sitting still: They were at peace.

Elizabeth didn't think she was figuring this all out on her own. Somehow, it felt as if the spectacles were guiding her interpretations.

"Halt!"

The dragon jumped at the unexpected sound of a voice from behind them. So did the girl. They had both been so preoccupied with the scene across the valley, they hadn't heard footfalls approach from their backside. They hadn't noticed the stone stairway up the side of the mountain or the cave that led inside it. They were so intent on preserving the element of surprise, they had not even considered the possibility of being caught by surprise themselves.

"Halt!" the voice repeated.

"We're not moving," said the dragon.

Elizabeth opened the invisible bubble barrier over her sleigh and climbed out. The air here so high on the mountain was even colder, if possible, than it had been at the North Pole Village. But even as the chill air sought to burrow its way up inside her wool-and-velvet coat, her attention was consumed by the stout and sturdy figure before her, who held an impressive spear, tipped with a large obsidian point. That point was just a few inches from Elizabeth's chest.

She backed up a step, and the spearpoint followed.

The girl studied the person on the other end. A gray-white parka, thick pants, heavy boots, and a cream-colored wool scarf covered every bit of skin except the newcomer's amber eyes. But perhaps most significant was the color of the aura that emanated from the spear-wielder. It was not black, like the aura around the cold-hearted thieves on the balloon ships; it was gray. She'd seen that color around some of the others, and she had thought it might mean the person was on the way to turning black. Perhaps that was so, she admitted, but there was something else, as well—something closer to the truth of it: There was sadness. She could see it behind the person's eyes. And this close, she could *feel* as well as see it. It felt like a waterfall of tears, held back by a dam of pure conviction. Without the spectacles, she would never have noticed it; with them, it was impossible to ignore.

"You are our prisoners," the newcomer said, her voice cool and steely.

Yes, it was a "her." Elizabeth had thought the voice was a woman's when she first heard it, but she hadn't been sure. Now she was, though.

"I would be careful where you point that thing, if I were you," Dreqnir warned. His voice was just as cool, but with an undercurrent of warning. "You are one small human. I am one rather substantial *dragon*." To illustrate his point, he reared his head back and sent a fountain of flame into the air. A few sparks came flickering and fluttering downward, fizzling as they hit the snowy ground.

"*I* would be careful if I were *you*," the spear-wielder countered. "You are not our only prisoners. We hold your mother, as well. If I do not return, he will know why, and your queen will pay the price."

"We? He?" Dreqnir snorted. "I see only you. You're bluffing. I don't think anyone else even knows you're here."

"He knows. He sees," the woman said simply.

"She's telling the truth," said Elizabeth. She knew because the spectacles were telling her so. Not verbally; it was just a feeling. But it was as plain as the evernight sky was dark.

Dreqnir eyed her skeptically, then sighed.

Elizabeth looked back at the woman. "What is your name?" she asked.

"That is unimportant."

"You are *not* unimportant," Elizabeth countered. "I believe you are very, very important indeed."

The woman said nothing.

"My name is Elizabeth."

The woman moved her mouth slightly, forming syllables that were barely audible: "Illian."

"I am pleased to meet you, Illian," said Elizabeth. "Why are you sad?"

The spearpoint quivered slightly, because the woman's hand shook. She was young, Elizabeth could tell, barely more than a child herself. "I am not sad," she said as evenly as possible, but Elizabeth heard her voice quiver, ever so slightly, as well.

"I know you are," said Elizabeth. "I can tell. You are alone."

"I am *not*," the spearmaiden protested, louder and more emphatically. "He is always with me. He sees me.

He knows me."

"And that makes you feel more alone," Dreqnir said.

The girl did not answer.

"Who is this 'he'?"

"Father Time," Illian said.

"Nigel," Dreqnir snorted. "I should have known."

"It is not your place to speak his name!" Illian nearly shouted.

Elizabeth took another step backward.

She shouldn't have.

She didn't know she was standing near the edge of the stone outcropping, which was the only thing separating her feet from the valley far below. As one of her feet met with air, she stumbled and tried to right herself, but she was so badly off-balance she couldn't keep herself from starting to fall. Pebbles dislodged from the outcropping skittered and fell toward the ground thousands of feet beneath her. She felt everything give way, and in the same instant, she saw Illian thrust the spearpoint forward.

Instinctively, the girl reached out with flailing arms, her fingers finding the wooden spear and wrapping themselves around it.

Holding on.

Desperately.

She felt herself being pulled back upward until her knees sank into the snow that blanketed the outcropping: solid ground.

She let go of the spear and bent forward, head in hands.

And began to weep.

"I just... want to... go home," she cried, tears running down her face from behind her magical glasses between sobs. The spectacles themselves were fogging up so that she couldn't see anything but the white of the snow and the black of the sky. "I... can't do this anymore."

She felt a gloved hand grasp hers and pull her to her feet.

"Yes, you can." Illian's voice was soft but determined. "If I can, you can, too."

Elizabeth took off the spectacles and wiped her eyes with her own gloved hand, meeting Illian's eyes. There was something more than sadness there now. There was sympathy. She knew that in a flash it would be gone, and the spear would be pointed at her once again, so she asked:

"How? How do you do it? Stay strong?"

Illian stood up straighter. "By knowing two things: That I am living today, and that tomorrow might be better."

"Yes." Elizabeth sniffed and nodded. "Just that."

"But we must not forget our yesterdays," said Dreqnir.

Illian nodded but did not answer him directly. "This

way," she said.

Elizabeth noticed she did not raise her spear again, but instead walked ahead of them, trusting them to follow. They were no longer her prisoners, though she did not admit as much directly. If Lord Nigel truly had the means to watch them, Elizabeth understood why.

Illian led them down a few steps and into the cave they had missed seeing before. A passage led them downward through a narrow space in a kind of crooked spiral—narrow, at least, for a dragon of Dreqnir's size. He had to slither along like a snake on his belly to make it through some of the closer quarters. Lanterns lit the way at regular intervals, casting shadows against the gray stone rock. It was warmer here than on the outside, and Elizabeth was glad to be beyond the reach of the chill, high Nordic wind. She wondered if they were being led into a trap, but the spectacles hadn't alerted her of any danger and, when she glanced at the compass, it showed they were going in the right direction: toward where the Dragon Queen was being held. What the compass couldn't tell her was how close—or far away—she was.

"Where are we?" Elizabeth asked.

"Underfall," Illian said, without further explanation. Elizabeth wondered why it might be called that, but she didn't ask. She sensed that Illian only had patience for a few questions, and she wanted to make sure the ones she posed were important.

As she was thinking this, one popped into her head that she sensed *was* important.

"Where is your family?"

"Dead," said Illian, her voice cold.

"What happened to them?"

"I don't know. When he brought me here, he told me his brother, Nicholas, took them away because I had been bad. He said he would make Nicholas pay for taking them away, and if I was good and did what he told me, he might be able to find them."

"Liar!" Dreqnir roared, rearing up and bumping his head on the roof of the tunnel. They had come to a wider less-cramped section of the tunnel, but the ceiling was still low enough that he had to crouch down slightly for it to accommodate his massive frame.

"Ouch," he said.

Elizabeth stopped and grabbed hold of Illian's hand, forcing her to stop, too. "It doesn't work like that," she said. "Dreqnir's right. Nigel has been lying to you."

Illian tried to pull away from Elizabeth and opened her mouth to protest—but said nothing. The girl held her hand fast. "I'm not going to let you go," Elizabeth said. "I know you have a good heart."

Illian stopped struggling. "*How* do you know?" she said finally.

Elizabeth was tempted to tell her about the

spectacles, but decided it was best that she keep that to herself for now.

"You could have let me fall over that cliff, but you didn't. You saved me."

"Hmmph," said Illian. "Reflexes."

Elizabeth smiled a half-smile and waited for the more important question.

At last it came: "And how do you know Father Time is lying to me?"

"Because he doesn't care about you, or anyone, being away from their family. If he did, he wouldn't have taken Dreqnir's mother from him."

The dragon bowed his head and half-closed his eyes.

"And he would not have taken Nicholas from his wife. She is so worried now because she does not know where he is. All she wants is for him to be back home with her."

Illian's eyes narrowed. "He deserved to be taken because of what he did to my parents!"

Dreqnir raised his head again. "Or what Nigel did himself and blamed on Nicholas," the dragon said. "You only blame Nicholas because of something Nigel told you. Did he show you any proof?"

"No..." Illian admitted slowly. "But he took me in. He has been nothing but kind to me."

"As kind as your parents were?" the dragon pressed her.

"I don't remember," she said coldly. "He told me to forget about them."

"I thought he told you he would try to find them for you," Elizabeth said.

"He did." Illian looked confused. "I don't know."

What else had he told her? Elizabeth remembered something she had said earlier: that Nigel somehow magically knew what Illian was doing. Elizabeth had seen what Nigel could do and had accepted it at face value. More important, the spectacles had told her that Illian was telling the truth when she'd said he was watching her every move. But what if she only *thought* she was telling the truth? What if she *believed* it was the truth, but it wasn't? The spectacles might not be able to tell the difference.

"You said he knows you're here," Elizabeth said. "You said he's always with you and can see what you're doing. How do you know?"

"What do you mean?"

"I mean, how do you know?" Elizabeth repeated.

"Because he told me."

Dreqnir's eyes widened slightly, and he seemed suddenly more alert. "Another lie," he said as the realization dawned on him. "He does *not* know we're here. If he did, he would have heard what we've been saying—and sent his guards to stop us."

Illian stiffened, tightening her grip on the spear. "Are

you saying he does not trust me to keep you in my custody?"

"He trusted you to trick us into going with you, and he trusted us to fall for it," Dreqnir said. "It almost worked. Almost."

He nodded toward Elizabeth. "I believe we still have the element of surprise on our side."

His tail whipped around in an instant and knocked the spear from Illian's grip. It went rattling over the floor of the tunnel and off into a darkened corner.

Illian lunged for it, but a giant dragon paw slammed down on the floor between her and the weapon.

She shouted in rage.

"Wait!" cried Elizabeth.

The two both stopped and looked at her.

"I think we should let her have it," the girl said.

"What?" The dragon was bewildered.

"I think she should have it," Elizabeth repeated. "I trust her."

"But why...?"

"You said it yourself. She really thought Nigel could see everything she was doing, *but she helped us anyway*."

Dreqnir nodded begrudgingly.

"She trusted Nigel, but something inside her told her she shouldn't. That's why she helped us. But she doesn't trust us, either. Why should she? She doesn't know us at all!"

The dragon nodded. He could see what she was thinking.

"So, if we trust *her*, we give her a reason to trust *us*," he said.

Elizabeth jumped excitedly and clapped. "Yes!" she said, clambering up and across the dragon's paw and retrieving the spear. After laying hold of it, she clambered back the other way and strode up to Illian.

She handed her the spear. "This is yours," she said.

Illian looked even more confused than before, but she finally said simply, "Thank you."

As Elizabeth watched, she saw the spearmaiden's aura change from gray to yellow-gold.

Chapter Sixteen

Piping Up

The sound of the flute's music filled the Minute-Hour's prison. The lilting melody was hypnotic and seemed to draw all those within the sound of it closer.

Ruffus stopped sniffing around the edges of the enclosure.

Alex stepped back toward the table, as well.

Isis purred and jumped down from his shoulder, padding silently across the floor toward Asterion, her eyes opening and closing sleepily.

"What *is* that tune?" the feline asked.

Asterion didn't answer her; he just kept playing.

And his three guests kept moving toward him in a stupor, even as something inside of Alex tugged at the back of his mind, trying to warn him.

A flute.

A flute.

Where had he heard about a flute?

Had it not been for the music, he would have known immediately. But the tune was crowding everything else out of his mind, leaving room for it alone. There was something magical about it that kept all other thoughts at bay. Absently, he reached into his pocket, and his hand found the Lou Gehrig baseball card. It was a reminder that, no matter what, he had to keep trying. No matter how long it took. If Lou Gehrig could play in more than 2,100 consecutive baseball games, he—Alex—could play *this* magical game to its conclusion. As these thoughts entered his head, they shattered the music's spell over him, and he remembered: The Flute of Pan's Third Daughter! It was the talisman he'd been looking for, and now, fortuitously, he'd stumbled upon it.

Of course, there was the problem of being stuck here at the center of the maze, but having the talisman was better than not having it... if he could get it away from the Minute-Hour.

That was a big "if."

He realized Asterion was using the flute to draw him forward, most likely so he could catch and eat him. He also realized that, if the Minute-Hour thought he was still under the music's spell...

The boy kept moving forward at a slow and steady pace, maintaining the same placid expression on his face and glazed look in his eyes. Asterion's attention was focused on the flute, his bull head bobbing slightly as his fingers danced over the holes in the instrument. Alex knew he would have to time things perfectly; the Minute-Hour was larger—much larger—than he was, and his plan would only work if he was quicker. He would have to make his move before Asterion raised his eyes.

He took a step. And then another. And then another, half-open eyes keenly focused on the bull-headed creature's face.

At the last possible moment, when it looked as if Asterion was about to raise his brow and look up, Alex leapt forward toward him.

The music stopped.

The boy's hand grabbed at the flute, but his fingers failed him; instead, his hand knocked it away. It hit the floor with a CLANG, then skidded across the tiles, coming to rest on the tail of a stylized dolphin embedded in the floor mosaic.

Asterion jumped to his feet, upending the table and knocking Alex to one side.

"Ruffus!" Alex cried.

The bloodhound bounded toward the flute and picked it up between his teeth.

The bull-headed man turned from Alex and ran after the bloodhound. He would have reached him in a few short moments if it hadn't been for Isis. The cat, roused from the stupor caused by the flute's music, jumped between the Minute-Hour and the canine—who was snarling as viciously as he could manage with the flute between his teeth—and began whirling her nine tails like a pinwheel in front of him.

The sight of it seemed to mesmerize Asterion, much as the flute's tune had mesmerized the three of them. Except it had the added effect of making the bull-headed man grow dizzy. As Alex watched, he seemed to teeter like a top as it slowed its spinning. He put both hands to his head, and then, when he could endure it no longer, collapsed to his knees and fell forward, sprawled out on the floor in front of them.

The boy stared at him, waiting for him to move.

He didn't.

"Is he...?"

"Asleep? Yes. One of my many talents," Isis boasted, her tails flicking this way and that.

Alex tried not to look at them.

Ruffus trotted up and dropped the flute at the boy's feet.

Alex picked it up and studied it closely: It had been crafted in silver and decorated with diamonds. He had no idea how to play the flute—or any instrument, for that matter—but he put it to his mouth and blew even so, experimenting. Much to his surprise, the sound that emerged was sweet and melodious, and remained so as he covered the holes, one after another, and then in combination, while continuing to play.

"Be careful with that," said Isis. "I have no desire to be hypnotized again!"

"Nor do I," Ruffus put in.

Alex stopped playing. "Who was Pan's third daughter, anyway?" he asked.

"Pan was the master of the woodland and its creatures," Isis said. "His first two daughters were given in marriage to the Sun King, Apollo, and to Silenus, king of the fauns. But his third daughter, Alera, remained unmarried. One day, when she was searching for a book in her father's study, she came upon her father's plans for the flute, which he had drawn up but seemed to have abandoned.

"She removed the plans and took them with her, deciding then and there that she would execute them herself. When she had done so, she placed a spell upon the instrument, intending that it should attract her one true love, so that she could be married like her sisters. But the spell went awry, and instead of calling forth a high lord or noble soldier, the flute would instead entice any who might hear it.

"The first person who did so was Narcissus, who

was already in love with his own beauty. Unable to reconcile his own self-love with the spell that bound him to Alera, he cast a spell of his own and transformed her into a man of his own likeness. Even this, however, failed to satisfy him, so he ridiculed Alera and refused to even call her by her name. Instead, he fashioned for her a multicolored suit and banished her to the town of Hamelin in lower Germany. There, she—or he—made a living by luring rats away from the town.

"When the mayor reneged on his agreement to pay for these services, the man who had once been Alera took his vengeance by using the pipe to lure away the village children."

Alex shook his head. "I've heard that story," he said. It made sense, except for one thing: He'd heard the story of the Minotaur, too, and it has supposedly happened hundreds of years earlier. It made no sense that Asterion should have come into possession of the flute *after* the Pied Piper had possessed it. Then again, he had always thought both tales were just made-up stories, so he supposed that having things out of order was no stranger than the stories being true in the first place.

"What happened to Alera?" the boy asked.

"The Piper felt such remorse for having separated the children of Hamelin from their parents, that she tossed it into the River of Time, and it washed up many hundreds of years earlier on the shores of Crete."

That explained how time had turned around.

Isis continued: "Asterion discovered it and hid it in his coat before he was banished to the labyrinth. I had forgotten all about that part of the story until he took it out and began to play. By then, it was too late for me to keep from falling under its spell. It's a good thing you were somehow immune to it, or you would have been roasting over a fire by now."

"Thanks," said Alex. He did not find that reminder the least bit comforting. "Do you think that was the River of Time—the river that we crossed before we came here?"

"It must have been," said Ruffus. "That would explain why time is so off-kilter here."

Alex sighed. It was bad enough not knowing where he was, but now he didn't know *when* he was, either.

"But what do we do now?" he asked. "And what do we do with him?" He pointed at the bull-man.

Isis yawned and purred at the same time, creating an odd sort of humming-rumbling sound. "He'll wake up eventually," she said. "When he does, I'll just put him back to sleep again. Besides, by that time, Ruffus will have found a way out. He's always bragging that he can find *anything*, and as much as I enjoy teasing him, I've never seen him fail." Her tone actually contained a hint of admiration.

Just a hint.

"Oh, thanks," said Ruffus sarcastically. "You had to choose this particular time to compliment me."

"What's wrong with this time?" Alex asked.

"Because for once, I can't find what I'm looking for. I just don't see a way out."

Chapter Seventeen

Tick Tock

"This way," said Illian.

They had come quite a long way, and Elizabeth could feel the soles of her feet aching all the way up her legs. She also felt the point of the spear at her back, sharp between her shoulder blades. Illian had told her they would be entering a "secure area" under heavy guard, so they would need to look convincing. She just wished they didn't need to be *this* convincing.

Indeed, they had started to encounter others in the caverns, which were warmer, better lit and more spacious here. Dreqnir looked happy to be able to walk at his full height, without crouching, at long last.

Guards, all armed with spears or equipped with

broadswords, passed them at regular intervals; some of them escorted prisoners, all of them nodded at Illian as they went their way.

Elizabeth wished she could turn around and look at the spearmaiden through the Spectacles of Samwell Spink one more time, just to be doubly sure she was still on their side. But each time she tried to look over her shoulder, the spear point dug more deeply into her back—even when they were alone.

Tunnels branched off in several directions, disappearing into darkness as they entered a series of catacombs. They stayed in the main passageway, which was lined with iron-barred cells, some empty, others occupied by prisoners of various shapes, sizes, and species. A large polar bear prowled back and forth inside one of the larger enclosures, muttering something under his breath about the prospect of vengeance. Elizabeth wondered if he was related to the family of bears she'd met at the North Pole. Farther on, a group of several black-clad pirates huddled in another cell, apparently hatching some conspiracy. They glanced up at the three of them as they passed, taking particular note of Dreqnir, before returning to the task at hand.

Elizabeth had decided it was best to keep the map and Compass of the Seventh Kingdom safely hidden, alongside the Pearly Pocketwatch underneath her coat. She removed the Spectacles of Samwell Spink and placed them there, too. The four talismans were all too valuable to be kept in plain sight, and she didn't want to take the chance of consulting them to find out whether they were on the right track.

"Turn here," said Illian as they came to a branch in the tunnel that forked off to the right.

So, they did.

And soon they found themselves at a heavily barred gate, guarded by a pair of speared sentinels.

Illian raised the spear and shoved Elizabeth roughly forward—so roughly that she stumbled and fell to one knee.

She got up slowly.

One of the guards nodded sharply toward Illian and stepped back, opening the gate.

"So, this is the dragonspawn," he said. "You are expected. You may pass."

Now Elizabeth was really starting to worry. The aura around both the sentinels was dark black. But, worse than that, they seemed to have *known* the three of them were coming. Had she been wrong about Illian? Had the spearmaiden been telling the truth when she'd said Nigel knew where they were and what they were up to? But how *could* he have known?

Magic.

The voice inside her head was not her own. It was Dreqnir's, speaking through the heart-gem. She could sense the worry in his thoughts, and this he now made explicit: *We have been tricked. It's a trap.*

Elizabeth was worried he was right. But there was nothing for it now: It was too late to turn back. She braced herself for what lay ahead as she heard the iron gate clang shut behind them. They were locked in; even if Illian hadn't lain a trap for them intentionally, they were, in fact, trapped now... unless there was another way out.

A few paces on, they came to more iron bars, laid across the opening to a very large recess in the rock.

Behind those bars stood a familiar figure.

The Dragon Queen.

Seeing her now, Elizabeth marveled anew at how perfect Lord Nigel's disguise had been at *Dragehjem.* She could not tell the difference between the imposing figure that stood before her and the illusion "Father Time" had crafted. Four guards stood in front of the bars, each armed with a long, imposing spear that was pointed through the bars at the Dragon Queen.

Dreqnir roared loudly.

"Open it," Illian commanded.

The guards complied.

She must be their superior, Dreqnir remarked in silent thought. Then, aloud, he said, "Mother, it is good to see you."

"I wish it could have been under different

circumstances," she said.

"Indeed. But we've come to get you out of here."

For the first time, Elizabeth was able to look at Illian again through the spectacles. Her aura was no longer gray or yellow, but copper. What could that mean? Worry? Inner conflict? It was something like that, she sensed, but she couldn't be quite sure; and she didn't know, either, what was causing it.

"Come here, my son. Let me see you," the Dragon Queen said.

Dreqnir stepped forward, into the cage... and the Dragon Queen dealt him a mighty blow with a gigantic wing. It knocked him against the back of the cage, dazing him as his mother began to change. Slowly vanishing. Growing smaller and taking on a different form.

Again.

In her place stood Lord Nigel. Before Dreqnir could recover, the Time Master raised his staff and called forth a bolt of lightning that froze the dragon in place, unmoving.

"Close the gate!" he cried as he leapt out of the cage. As he did so, he lowered his staff, and Dreqnir lunged after him... but too late. The guards slammed the gate in his face, his head smashing hard against unyielding iron.

Nigel surveyed his work, a satisfied look on his face. "Well done!" he declared, turning to Illian with a broad smile.

Dreqnir howled in rage.

"Now we have both of them: the monarch and her heir. We have the means to bring the Dragon Home to its knees."

Illian shot an ever-so-brief sidelong glance at Elizabeth. There was something in her eyes—apologetic, but also a hint of surprise. She hadn't known this was coming. She hadn't betrayed them, after all.

Elizabeth racked her brain, then it came to her: The guards they had passed in the catacombs must have alerted Nigel to their presence. But Nigel thought they had done so at Illian's behest.

Elizabeth nodded back discretely. They still had a chance.

In a single, fluid motion like a flash of lightning, Illian raised her spear and thrust it at Lord Nigel.

But Nigel was quicker. He vanished in a flash, then reappeared behind her and wrapped an arm around her neck.

"You thought you could trick me!" he laughed, his mad voice echoing through the chamber. "Didn't your friend here tell you? I know *everything*. Past, present, and every possible future. I am its author and its master. A dragon, a girl, and a traitor"—he glared at Illian—are no match for me."

"You're lying." Elizabeth was surprised at how sure of this she was. It wasn't something she had to convince herself was true. She *knew* it.

That was when she felt it inside her coat.

At first, she thought it was Dreqnir trying to reach her through the heart-gem, but it wasn't that. It was something else.

Tick.

Tock.

Tock.

Tick.

The Pearly Pocketwatch. She'd almost forgotten she had it. It was trying to tell her something, but she had no way of knowing what. All she wished was that she could go back in time a few minutes with the knowledge she had now. She wished that more than anything.

She heard Lord Nigel shout, "Guards, seize her!" and she saw two big men advancing toward her.

But before they could reach her, everything spun away in a dizzying kaleidoscope of sound and color that seemed backward from the way it should have been. She closed her eyes tightly, lost her balance, and felt herself falling to the ground, but somehow, she never hit it. Instead, when she opened her eyes, she was glancing over at Dreqnir, who somehow stood beside her.

His voice was speaking through the heart-gem. "*We have been tricked. It's a trap.*"

They were back where they had been before, just inside the first gate.

Somehow, the pocketwatch had sent them back there. She'd wished to go back in time a few minutes, and it had granted her that wish. It had given them a second chance.

"*Yes, it is a trap. I know*, Elizabeth answered. *Nigel is waiting for us in there, disguised as your mother. He plans to trick you into entering a cage, then trap you in there and take us all prisoner. Illian doesn't know any of this. She's still on our side.*"

Dreqnir looked at her, puzzled. "*How do you know?*"

"*I've seen it. It already happened.*"

The dragon looked even more baffled.

"*Trust me. I don't have time to explain. They're going to take us to your mother. Only it's not her. It's Nigel. So when he asks you to enter the cage...*"

Dreqnir nodded. "*Got it.*"

Everything happened then just the same way it had happened before. They approached the giant cage that held what appeared to be the Dragon Queen. But Elizabeth decided to don the spectacles again this time, and saw they revealed the blackest aura she had seen around the "dragon." She was angry at herself for having removed them the first time, because they would have revealed the truth. But at least now, she had a second chance. She would have to make the most of it.

She only wished she knew what to do. She had used the Pearly Pocketwatch to reset time, without even knowing what she was doing. Somehow, the watch itself seemed to have guided her—just as the spectacles had shown her the meaning behind each aura they revealed. Perhaps the talismans would guide her again.

Even as she thought this, a question entered her head, seemingly out of nowhere: What if she could use the pocketwatch more selectively? What if, instead of sending everyone back to where they were before, it could be focused on just one person?

And what if that person were...?

"Open it," Illian said, just as she had before. And just as they had before, the guards complied.

She must be their superior, Dreqnir remarked, repeating the silent words he had uttered the first time. Then, aloud, he said, once again, "Mother, it is good to see you."

Only this time, he didn't mean it.

"I wish it could have been under different circumstances," came the response.

"Indeed. But we've come to get you out of here." Elizabeth saw a gleam in Dreqnir's eye, a sign that he meant something altogether different than he had the first time.

"Come here, my son. Let me see you," the false Dragon Queen said.

But this time, Dreqnir's response was different: "No, Mother," he replied. "You come to me. I cannot bear to see you in that cage any longer."

The figure inside the cage hesitated, taken aback by

this turn of events, then, seeing no other option, stepped forward beyond the bars.

Dreqnir stepped forward and threw his forearms and wings around "her" in a hearty embrace.

A tight embrace.

The "Dragon Queen" started to struggle, then began to shrink and change shape. But as her form got smaller, Dreqnir tightened his grip all the more, refusing to let go. Gradually, the image of Lord Nigel began to replace that of the giant dragon. Elizabeth was worried he might simply vanish, as he had before, but she heard Dreqnir's voice through the heart-gem, saying, *"He cannot perform two feats of magic at once. He cannot disappear until he regains his own true form."*

Elizabeth nodded. She knew she only had seconds to act. But in those seconds, all the time in the world was at her disposal.

She pulled out the Pearly Pocketwatch and thrust it out at arm's length toward Nigel.

He froze.

An expression of shock seemed carved into his face as he stood there, nearly himself again except for a scaly residue of faux dragon skin that covered him from head to toe. Illian stood gawking, a similar expression on her face. One of the guards pointed his spear at Dreqnir, only to be met by a billowing flame that singed his beard and left his face black with soot. He dropped the spear and fainted. His three cohorts just stood there, unsure of what to do.

"You can let him go now," Elizabeth said to Dreqnir, who dropped Nigel's rigid form unceremoniously and watched it clang to the ground like a silver tray. His mouth was still agape and his eyes wide in what had become a perpetual look of astonishment. The master of time had been mastered *by* time.

Dreqnir turned to the guards. "Where is she?" he demanded in a booming voice. "Take us to the *real* Dragon Queen!"

Illian had dropped the pretense. Her spear was no longer at Elizabeth's back; instead, she was using it to herd the guard who had "volunteered" to take them to the Dragon Queen. The other guards they passed in the catacombs didn't dare confront them; Dreqnir made sure of that. Any who dared raise spear or sword against them found their weapons burned and melted by a blast of dragon fire.

They found the Dragon Queen—the *real* Dragon Queen—in a massive dungeon blocked by a giant rock. It had been sealed by a form of magic, so even Dreqnir couldn't move it. Fortunately, the guard they had conscripted to their cause knew the spell that was needed to release it, much as a combination releases the lock to a safe. He resisted at first, but when Elizabeth pulled out the pocketwatch and showed it to him, he relented: He clearly had no desire to share his master's fate.

"How long will he remain like that?" Illian had asked when they'd left Nigel lying there.

Elizabeth had shrugged. She had no idea. She only hoped the effect would last long enough for them to find the Dragon Queen, locate King Nicholas, and make their escape.

Once inside, Dreqnir embraced his mother and introduced her to Elizabeth and Illian. Her proper name, they found out, was Queen Taradreq, and she was extremely grateful to be rescued from her confinement. She was even more grateful to see her son, who she had feared was lost to her when Tar Kidron had used their bond to force him into servitude. It had been years since the two had seen each other, and, in fact, it had been Dreqnir's bond to Tar Kidron that had led to Taradreq's captivity. Nigel had appeared to her and had threatened to harm Dreqnir if she resisted. He had pledged to release her son from his bond with Tar Kidron, but instead had imprisoned her here, beneath this mountain.

"Do you know where King Nicholas has been taken?" Elizabeth asked.

The queen shook her head. "I have seen nothing of this place, save for the inside of this cell."

"Then perhaps it is time to do some exploring,"

Dreqnir said with a wink.

Illian smiled broadly. “I can be your guide.”

CHAPTER EIGHTEEN

Fire in the Sky

Elizabeth awoke to what sounded like a distant ringing in her ears. Ringing? Not quite. It sounded less like a bell and more like something else. It was so faint, however, that she couldn't quite put her finger on it. She shook her head, and it seemed to abate.

She groaned as she sat up straight. Even as young as she was, her muscles ached after a night of "rest" on solid rock, and she was homesick for her own bed. How long had it been since she'd slept there? She'd lost count of the days amid the unending darkness—if days even had any meaning here. They'd caught a few hours of shuteye in a dark recess Illian had shown them; the guards passed by it but either ignored it or didn't realize it was there.

Elizabeth had hoped the darkness might abate once Nigel was frozen in time, but she had no such luck: Carol had been right in saying that the evernight was something more pernicious than even "Father Time" could summon.

The girl, the spearmaiden, and the two dragons had made their way through the passages inside the mountain. Guards and soldiers buzzed this way and that; it was clear from their nervousness and the words exchanged between them that news of their master's "condition" had spread. If they stopped long enough to take note of the four travelers, the sight of two large dragons was enough to make them look the other way. They were entirely in disarray, uncertain of what to do or where to go without Lord Nigel's guidance.

Illian, on the other hand, seemed to know exactly where she was going. It helped, of course, that Elizabeth held a magical map and compass, but the map was of little use in such close quarters, so it was up to Illian to navigate the tunnels and keep the compass needle pointing forward. Speaking of close quarters, they had to take the long way around more than once in order to find tunnels large enough for the two dragons to pass. It had been enough of a challenge traveling with Dreqnir, but Taradreq's frame was even larger.

Despite several detours, they finally found their way out of the mountain, stepping through a massive oaken door and out onto a high plateau that stretched away from the side of the mountain.

The plateau was covered with snow—more of it than Elizabeth had ever seen this close, even at the North Pole.

Her feet felt colder than they ever had before. She wondered why at first, but then she understood: They were standing on a glacier. She moved slightly and felt her feet slip, then she slid and tumbled unceremoniously backward onto her posterior.

"Careful," said Dreqnir.

"Little late for that," Illian quipped, smirking.

The girl scowled, dusted off her backside, and rose to her feet. She looked up at the night sky, bejeweled with countless twinkling stars, and found some comfort in seeing the *Revontulet*—the Northern Lights—off in the distance once again. It occurred to her that the evernight was keeping the glacier ice from melting even a little, preserving it in the absence of the sunlight that would typically warm it.

The good news was that a near-full moon was out, and its light reflected off the ice to provide a clear view of what lay before them: the balloon city. They had descended a bit within the mountain and found themselves much closer to it now, looking straight across at it rather than down from near the summit.

Elizabeth glanced at the compass: It pointed

straight ahead. Reaching up, she adjusted her spectacles to magnify the scene before her. The balloon ships, tethered to the plateau, floated silently on a lagoon of air, bobbing up and down in a slight, chill breeze. Few people seemed to be out and about; but Elizabeth saw a lone figure running—and occasionally slip-sliding—across the glacier a short distance ahead of them, moving toward the ship-city.

It was one of the guards from inside the mountain.

He finally came to a stop at a gangplank that connected the plateau to the nearest ship, where he started speaking and gesturing frantically to a crew member who had strolled up to meet him.

"They're relaying the news of Nigel's... predicament," Dreqnir said.

Elizabeth turned to him, puzzled.

"We dragons have exceptional ears," he explained. "We can hear the first tiny icefall from miles away, before it becomes an avalanche."

"Don't exaggerate," Taradreq chided, but there was laughter behind her mock-serious tone.

Dreqnir, however, did not share her mirth. "Exaggeration has helped keep us alive, Mother. Would-be enemies who think us more fearsome than we are tend to keep their distance."

Taradreq changed her tone to match his earnestness. "As do would-be friends. Elizabeth and Illian are our friends, are they not?"

Dreqnir stayed silent, but Elizabeth felt something that seemed like embarrassment through the heart-gem.

The girl kept her eyes on what was happening aboard the ship. The guard stepped aboard, and the crew member who had met him dashed away, disappearing through a door that led belowdecks. Within moments, the sleepy ship became a hive of activity, which spread like wildfire to the other ships anchored near the mountain.

"We must hurry," said Taradreq. "They know something's wrong, and they will be scrambling to weigh anchor and depart. Thieves and swindlers do not like anything that brings them attention, and they will want to find a safer haven than one where the master is... indisposed."

"Are you sure King Nicholas is aboard those ships?" asked Illian.

"The needle is pointing that way," said Elizabeth. "But I don't know. He could be farther away, on the other side of the valley. I don't know how to tell."

"He's there," said Dreqnir. "I can smell him."

"Don't tell me dragons have a heightened sense of smell, too," said Illian.

"Actually, we do," the dragon said. "But in this case, it's a figure of speech. I was bound to Tar Kidron for many years. I learned how he thinks, and because he was

Nigel's lieutenant, I know how 'Father Time' thinks, as well." He nodded toward the ship in front of them, then looked at Elizabeth. "That ship is a slaver's ship, isn't it?"

Elizabeth nodded. It was the same ship she had seen from above—the one where they had been auctioning people on a podium. The thought of it disgusted her.

"I thought so. It's configured to accommodate people, not just crated goods, belowdecks. And I *can* smell the scent of them, even this far away." He sneered. "Slavers are not known for taking good care of the men and women they've abducted."

"I can vouch for that," Taradreq said. "But how do you know King Nicholas is aboard?"

Dreqnir frowned. "Lord Nigel does not merely covet his brother's throne, he resents and even despises him. Nothing would please him more than to reduce him to the lowest state possible. And who is lower than a slave?"

"Slavery has been outlawed for years in England," said Elizabeth. "Even the Americans have ended it. How is it still practiced here?"

"Illegally," Dreqnir snorted. "And the Americans haven't really ended slavery. They still jail and shun and scorn people because of the color of their skin. They still make poor people work in sweatshops and call it an 'honest living.' There's nothing honest about it, and it isn't living. It's barely even surviving."

"I hope the twentieth century is better," said

Elizabeth.

"We shall see," said Dreqnir. He did not sound hopeful.

"Do you think they will take Nicholas to America?" said Illian.

Dreqnir shook his head. "No one knows. Once slaves are taken aboard these ships, no one knows where they end up. The sky pirates make it almost impossible to track them. They change their names and demand that they forget their past, on pain of torture to the point of death. It's highly effective."

"Then we have to hurry," said Elizabeth.

"Didn't I just say that?" Taradreq put in.

"What do you suggest, Mother?" asked Dreqnir. "We have been relying on the element of surprise since we arrived, and we nearly got ourselves captured."

The Dragon Queen nodded and bared her teeth. Elizabeth couldn't tell whether it was a smile or a look of menace.

"I suggest," she said, "we make an *entrance*!"

Illian climbed aboard Taradreq, Elizabeth fastened herself into the sleigh on Dreqnir's back, and the two dragons took to the sky. There was no hiding now amid the bright moonlight, and in no time at all, the people scurrying about on the airships below had caught sight of them.

They began to scurry all the more.

Cries of "Dragon!" and "Sky demon!" and "Ahoy! Look up!" filled the air.

The dragons didn't stay aloft for long. They descended like blazing comets toward the ship, announcing their approach with bursts of fire from mouths and nostrils before landing with a thud that splintered timbers on the deck, which sagged beneath their substantial weight. Crew members scrambled away, seeking refuge on masts and belowdecks; the few that stood their ground with broadswords retreated when the dragons turned to face them.

"Where is King Nicholas?" Illian demanded.

"Who wants to know?"

They turned at the sound of the voice behind them and found themselves facing a man of swarthy complexion with thick, wavy black hair and a full black beard. He wasn't particularly tall—no taller than Illian—or physically impressive: He stooped a little and had a paunch for a belly. But his eyes flashed strangely between ice blue and fire red, giving an impression of ire and volatility.

"His friends," said Elizabeth.

"Who you don't want as your enemies," Dreqnir added.

The black-haired man didn't seem daunted or even particularly impressed. He leaned casually against a mast that rose to the huge balloon overhead, crossing his feet and pretending to look intently at his drawn sword.

"And who are you?" asked Illian. "A thief? A pirate?"

"Yes, and yes," the man said, not bothering to look up from the sword. "A particularly skilled one, if I do say so myself, and the captain of this vessel on top of that. Welcome to my ship, the Tranquility."

"You're a pirate, then," said Taradreq.

"In a manner of speaking, although I prefer to think of myself as an entrepreneur and something of a philanthropist."

"A philanthropist?" Dreqnir snorted. "You captain a slave ship full of prisoners!"

"I was a prisoner myself once—the thanks I received for my philanthropy." He raised an eyebrow, then winked and grinned. Whatever he had endured, it seemed to have driven him mad. Or maybe that was just what he wanted them to think. "I planned the greatest heist of my career to benefit all of humankind. I succeeded—I always do—but had the misfortune of being discovered by the owner of the 'artifact' I plundered. When he got his hands on me, he had me chained to a rock and left to the elements. It was only after many years that I was rescued.

"But the humans who profited from my charity never sought to ease my pain, so I determined not to allay theirs, either. I do not 'own' the slaves aboard my ship;

they belong to other businessmen, who pay me well to take them here and there. They might as well be shipping silk or olive oil, for all I care. It is none of my concern. It is an honest exchange: my services for their gold. Some would find it more honorable than thievery, even theft for the sake of charity."

He *was* crazy, Elizabeth thought. She supposed that being chained to a rock and left out in the open for years might drive a man to madness, but knowing this hardly lessened her disgust. How could a self-proclaimed "philanthropist" captain a slave ship without any apparent shame? How could *anyone* dismiss his own role in such a heartless enterprise so casually?

As if reading her thoughts, he said, "Judge me if you will. It is no concern of mine. I have been judged a thousand times by creatures far more powerful than you."

"We shall see about that," Taradreq said, her voice low and menacing.

The thief just laughed.

"What is this artifact you stole?" asked Dreqnir.

"Oh, you will find out soon enough," said the thief.

"Enough of your games," the younger dragon said. He was clearly growing tired of the thief's cool audacity. "Where is King Nicholas?"

"I'm afraid I can't tell you that," said the thief. "I am bound by a contract with my client."

"I'm afraid," Dreqnir mocked, "you will *have to* tell us that."

"Or what?"

"Or this!" Dreqnir opened his mouth and blew hard just above the thief's head. It wasn't intended to hurt him, just to get his attention. The flames, he thought, might singe his hair a little, but he had it coming.

To his stunned surprise, however, nothing came out. Just hot air. No fire.

Chagrined, Dreqnir took a deep breath and blew again—with the same disappointing result.

Taradreq followed suit.

Nothing happened.

"Looking for something?" the thief teased. Then he balled up something in his fist and flung it suddenly at Dreqnir.

The fireball appeared and coalesced abruptly out of nowhere. Flying like a sparkling orange pinwheel through the air, it struck Dreqnir squarely in his chest and knocked him backward onto the deck.

Illiana raised her spear and flung it at the thief, but her target simply hurled another fireball at the weapon. The two projectiles met in midair, and the spear disintegrated into ash, leaving the sharp obsidian point to fall and rattle around on the deck.

"This will teach you to stand against Captain Prometheus!" the thief shouted gleefully.

Elizabeth had learned about Prometheus in her studies. He was a Greek titan who had, according to legend, stolen fire from Zeus in heaven and given it to humanity. For his trouble, he had been chained to a rock and sentenced to have his liver eaten by an eagle. The girl had found that part of the story rather disgusting, but she had always considered it just a *story*. Until now. It looked, to all appearances and against all odds, that this Captain Prometheus, whether he was the titan himself or a namesake, had succeeded in stealing fire from both the dragons.

He threw another fireball, this one at Taradreq, who tumbled backward and nearly off the ship.

Fortunately, the thief was all but ignoring Elizabeth, probably thinking she was too small to pose a threat. Sensing an opportunity, she reached frantically inside her coat and fumbled for the Pearly Pocketwatch. If she could use it against this mad thief the way she had used it against Lord Nigel, perhaps she could keep this from getting any worse. But instead of the pocketwatch, her fingers found the compass, which she proceeded to fumble in front of her on the deck.

This attracted the thief's notice, and he turned his attention toward her at last. Rearing back, he let fly a fireball straight in her direction—just as the girl bent down to retrieve the compass.

The fireball sailed directly over her head...

...and exploded into a thousand sparks against the mast directly behind her.

The mast, of course, was made of wood.

And wood, of course, is flammable.

So, unsurprisingly, it caught fire. One might have thought that Prometheus, being both the captain of a wooden ship and a wielder of fireballs, might have known the danger of unleashing such weapons at this proximity to flammable elements. Maybe he did, and maybe he didn't. Maybe he simply wasn't thinking. But whatever the case, the cool, unflappable expression on his face changed to one of alarm when he saw the flames catch hold on the mast and start licking their way upward toward the balloon.

A balloon filled with hydrogen gas.

Now, these events took place nearly a half-century before the famed Hindenburg dirigible—which was, likewise, filled with hydrogen—burst into flame and crashed in New Jersey. That accident might have been prevented had the airship used nonflammable helium, rather than combustible hydrogen, to stay aloft. Unfortunately, the Hindenburg wasn't allowed to use helium because the United States had a monopoly on the gas.

Hence, its tragic end.

And helium wasn't used to keep *any* airship aloft until the second decade of the twentieth century. At the close of the nineteenth century, when Elizabeth entered the labyrinth, no one was using helium for much of anything. It had only recently been discovered—which brings us back to the story at hand, and the fact that Prometheus' airship, like the Hindenburg, was kept floating near the clouds by hydrogen.

A highly flammable gas.

Prometheus turned his attention from Elizabeth to his crew, barking orders to gather buckets and fill them with water to douse the flames. Unfortunately, water is a lot harder to come by on an airship than it is in a traditional ship floating on the ocean, and there wasn't enough of it on board to stop the flames from spreading.

Elizabeth didn't know about hydrogen or helium, so she wasn't as worried as she might have been. At first, she was relieved that there weren't any actual *sails* to catch fire, as there would have been on a seagoing ship. But as the flames rose higher, and attempts to douse them failed, the crew members turned their attention to a different task: abandoning ship. They ran for the port gangplank connecting the ship with the glacier, or for the starboard plank connecting it to an adjacent ship, flagged as the Serenity. It, in turn, floated on air beside ships flagged as Concord and Equanimity. Elizabeth thought it strange that pirate airships should have such peaceful names. It was just another example of things that didn't make sense in this place.

On the port side, she saw men jumping and slipping onto the ice. One of them knocked the plank away, and it tumbled down to the valley below, forcing those who hadn't made it across to either try leaping over the gap or to flee in the opposite direction, to the adjacent airship.

Jumping toward the glacier was not an attractive option. Those few who tried couldn't find anything to grab except slippery ice and found themselves sliding backward, arms and legs flailing, off the mountain to their doom below.

The rest who had headed in that direction quickly thought better of it, and reversed course, making for the Serenity. There was much less peril in this course of action, at least initially, but as each of them landed on the deck of the neighboring vessel, it sagged ever so slightly beneath the added weight: It was hard to tell how much it could absorb.

Captain Prometheus was running this way and that, trying to persuade his crew not to abandon their posts. Most of them, however, had no interest in going down with the ship. More than half had already fled by the time another thought apparently occurred to the captain: "The cargo!" he shouted. "We can't just leave the cargo!"

Elizabeth realized he was talking about the slaves. They were stuck belowdecks, no doubt locked into cramped holds while they awaited possible buyers.

"The prisoners!" she cried. "We have to get them

out!"

Illian rushed toward the door that led belowdecks, but Prometheus barred her way. "No, you don't, Lassie," he said. "I've got too much invested in..."

He tried to form a fireball in his hand, then thought better of adding to the growing inferno. Instead, he threw his body across the door and dared her to try to get past him.

Illian took the dare. She punched him in the face, and he crumpled to the deck in a heap. She climbed over him and threw open the door.

"Wait!" Taradreq called. "I have a better idea."

She leapt and then soared skyward, causing the deck to shudder and rise as she relieved it of her weight. She banked sharply, then dove around the far side of the ship and flew straight toward it, slamming into it with all the force she could muster and causing splinters to fly where the sideboards had been.

Illian grabbed hold of the doorframe and held on tight to keep from falling as the ship shuddered and listed to one side. The gangplank between the Tranquility and Serenity flew skyward, then tumbled to the valley below, leaving the few crew members who hadn't escaped stranded aboard Prometheus' vessel. Elizabeth fell and slid sideways toward the edge, but Dreqnir caught her in his talons and flew eastward, setting her down briefly upon the glacier.

A moment later, she climbed into the sleigh on his back, and he ascended once again. From there, they could see a massive hole in the starboard bow of the ship, where the captives were waiting as Taradreq took them, several at a time, onto her back. When she could carry no more, she ferried her passengers across to the glacier, then returned to the ship for another load.

By this time, the other airships in the pirate armada were breaking free and rising into the air, having cut the ropes and straps that bound them to the earth below. It was a majestic sight to see them rising and moving away, fleeing the fires that were consuming the Tranquility. The flames had nearly reached the balloon above the ship, and Taradreq was hurrying to gather the last of the prisoners from the lower deck before it was too late. A young boy hesitated, looking scared. He crawled to the edge of the splintered boards, then clung to them, looking down, but unwilling to climb onto the dragon's back. Suddenly, with those already on her back holding tight, she rose and extended the talons from one massive claw, closing them tight around the boy and flapping her wings once mightily to push herself away.

In almost the same instant, the balloon overhead exploded in a massive fireball that made it almost seem like the sun had returned to reclaim the evernight sky. The ropes burned and snapped. The balloon deflated and disappeared in flame, and the ship, deprived of the gas that had been keeping it aloft, came crashing down, smashing into the side of the mountain and coming apart into splintered boards, some still aflame, that fell thousands of feet to the earth below.

Taradreq landed, out of breath, on the glacial plateau, setting the frightened boy down first and then allowing the other refugees to climb down from her back.

Dreqnir touched down beside her.

"Did you get everyone, Mother?" he asked.

"I think so," she said. "That one there was the last one." She nodded toward the boy, who was shivering and sobbing on the hard ice of the glacier.

Some of the former slaves talked excitedly, but many seemed badly shaken. A few wandered around, seemingly in a daze, but most eventually gathered into groups; some were obviously members of the same clan or village, having been taken together into captivity by the traders. The boy, however, was alone.

Elizabeth ran over to him and put an arm around him, raising him to his feet.

"What's your name?" she said. But he could not stop crying long enough to answer her.

"Are you here alone?"

He nodded, still sobbing.

Elizabeth glanced at the other airships, growing steadily smaller and disappearing beyond more distant mountains. She wondered if any other captives were aboard.

She turned back to the boy, who was looking up at her. He couldn't have been more than ten.

"I'm alone, too," she said.

He was shivering in the cold.

"We can be alone together," she said, "until we find our way home."

He nodded.

"I'm Elizabeth," she said, but he didn't answer.

Then she heard that ringing in her ears again—not a ringing, but a melody. It was still too faint to make it out, as though it wasn't coming from inside her head but very far away.

She turned to Dreqnir. "Do you hear that?"

"Hear what?" he asked her.

"I thought you said dragons had very good ears."

"The best," he said simply.

She shook her head, and the playing stopped. Perhaps she had imagined it. But then, a moment later, it began again.

Chapter Nineteen

Out of Time

"Are you sure you can't find a way out?" said Alex. He was growing hungry. The Minute-Hour didn't keep any food in his cupboards, relying solely on children for his sustenance.

Asterion had awakened twice now, and each time, Isis had waved her multiple tails and lulled him back to sleep.

Ruffus shook his head and howled a half-hearted, mournful howl. He had been sniffing and snuffing around all day, but he was no closer to finding the exit to Asterion's prison than he had been when he started.

"Do you have any ideas, Isis?"

The feline opened her eyes halfway and shook her

head lazily. She seemed oddly unconcerned, but cats always seemed that way, even in the direst situations. They seemed more interested in sleeping and grooming than anything else, and the boy wondered how they managed to survive with such a laissez-faire attitude in such a dangerous world. "Can't you *do* something?" he said.

She yawned. "I can do many things," she said sleepily. "But none of them will help, so the best thing I can do is conserve my energy."

"What if we all die in the meantime?"

"I have seven more lives," she said casually. "I'm not particularly worried."

"Well, I am!" Alex nearly shouted. "I only have one, and I don't want to see it end yet."

"If you want to do something constructive, why not play the Minute-Hour's flute?" Isis suggested.

"How is that constructive?"

"It's a magical flute," she stated simply. "Who knows what it can do?"

She had a point. Alex had thought about using the baseball card to escape, but he didn't know how that would help him. He had approached the wall with it and held it out in front of him, hoping against hope that the barrier might collapse and disappear, the way the Reaper had when he'd been confronted with the card. But it didn't work that way. The card had no effect at all on the barrier.

What the flute would do was anyone's guess. Alex remembered a Bible story about a hero and his soldiers who walked around a fortified city blowing trumpets, which somehow caused the walls to fall down before them. He started playing the flute, as Isis suggested, but the walls here seemed as solid as ever. He tried walking around in circles, but that didn't work, either. If the flute had any kind of magic, it wasn't the kind that made walls crumble or disappear.

Alex set the flute down.

"Keep playing," said Ruffus.

"But why? This thing won't get us out of here."

"I don't think it will, either," the bloodhound confessed. "But remember how it worked before, when Asterion played it?"

Alex shook his head. He had no idea what the dog was getting at.

"It called us to him," Ruffus explained.

Alex brightened. "Like the Pied Piper."

"Yes."

"We can't get out, but we *did* get in," Isis yawned. "Maybe if someone else hears the music, they can come and rescue us."

"If they don't get stuck in here, too," said Ruffus.

"Well, there is that," Isis conceded.

Alex nodded grimly. "It's better than nothing," he

decided, then put the flute to his lips again and resumed playing. He still had no idea how to play the flute, but the flute seemed not to care, and the tune that came out the other end of the instrument was one he had known for as long as he could remember: Brahms' Lullaby. His mother had hummed it to him in the cradle before he had been orphaned and begun his foster life—not that he recalled this exactly, but the memory had been there somewhere, all but lost inside the labyrinth of his mind. It comforted him, and it made him yearn for home.

But it occurred to him, then for the first time, that he didn't know where home really was.

Alex came from Iowa, with its red barns and cornfields, but he had never felt like he belonged there. It all seemed too *new* to him, which was strange for one so new to the world himself. In a sense, he had felt most at home on his first day of school: The classrooms and corridors felt familiar, as though he were supposed to be there. Almost. Even Moravia Elementary was not quite right. He had been bullied there, teased for being taller and quieter than the others, and the teasing had gotten worse when he refused to fight back against students who pushed him on the playground or cut in front of him in line.

He'd started missing school because of it, saying he had a sore throat or an earache just to avoid the taunts of other children. More and more, he'd just stayed in his room, teaching himself the things they should have been teaching him in school: *how* to learn, *where* to look for what he wanted to know, and *why* things were the way they were. Instead of learning from textbooks and lectures, he'd learned from novels and comic books, from old magazines in the attic, and from baseball cards that came collected in neatly wrapped packs. He'd read about the Depression and Pearl Harbor in the pages of *Time*, and he'd memorized the statistics of all the greatest ballplayers, enshrined on cardboard rectangles that smelled like bubblegum.

As time went on, he'd realized it wasn't just the bullying that made him feel out of place at the school.

It was the school itself.

He wasn't supposed to be there, *at that particular school*. He was supposed to be at a different school, where *he* could decide what subjects would be offered and how classes would be conducted. The strangest part of it all was that he could envision the school as if it really existed. Just not here. And not now.

Alex realized as he reflected on these things, that Iowa had never felt like home because, in a very real sense, it wasn't. His home was elsewhere, and he'd entered this maze to find it.

He remembered what the tree-man, Likho, had said to him: If he did not find his way home, past, present and future would become disconnected, and the entire world would be trapped in this maze that he had entered. What if the maze itself were like a school? What if it were a series of lessons, like classes, that he needed to learn in order to move on with his life?

But why should the whole world be caught up in this? That didn't make sense. What did make sense, though, was that something was very, very wrong—and that he needed to make it right. He just had no idea how. If he needed to find his way home, but Iowa was *not* that home, what exactly did he need to find?

He had reached the center of the maze, but now he needed to find his way out of a prison from which there was no escape.

He stopped playing the flute for a moment.

"Will everything always be this hopeless?" he said.

Isis purred softly. "You can choose to have hope or not," she said. "That is your choice, whatever your circumstances may be. You can accept them or try to change them. You can accept hope or discard it. The choice is yours."

Alex sighed. Even when he'd hidden in his room from those schoolyard bullies, he'd still had hope. He had felt trapped then, just as he did now, but he hadn't given up. So, he wouldn't give up now. He remembered the girl Likho had told him about, to whom he had sent the map and the compass, and realized he had given her a reason to hope. Perhaps someone he didn't know, someone beyond these walls, could give him such a reason in the same way.

He lifted the flute and started playing again, but this time, a different tune came out: one he didn't know. How or why he could play music he had never heard, he had no idea. But a title came into his head, as well: "Long, Long Ago."

The young boy from the Tranquility shook Elizabeth awake. They had returned to the catacombs inside the mountain, which offered them refuge from the freezing sub-Arctic air. The tunnels were empty now. Nigel's men seemed to have abandoned them, and when Elizabeth and the dragons returned to the place where they'd left "Father Time," they found him gone, as well. The girl only hoped he had been removed by his followers and hadn't awakened on his own.

She decided not to think about it. Either way, it was convenient that he and his men had gone. It gave the refugees from the Tranquility a place to stay while they waited to return home. Taradreq had pledged to help them get there, offering the services of her dragon subjects to fly them wherever they needed to go. Some, however, did not have homes. For some, their homes had been burned or destroyed by the men who had enslaved them; others had been taken as young children and had been slaves so long they didn't even know where "home" was.

Among the children from the Tranquility was the scared little boy that the Dragon Queen had plucked from the airship before it went up in flames.

Elizabeth still didn't know his name. All she knew was that, like her, he felt alone and wanted to find his way home.

She opened her eyes and found him staring at her.

"Why did you come here?" he asked.

"What?" Elizabeth sat up and rubbed the sleepy sand out of her eyes with her knuckles.

"Why did you come here?" the boy asked again.

"To find the Dragon Queen," she said, yawning, "and to free King..." Her voice trailed off.

To free King Nicholas.

With a start, she realized that she hadn't seen Nicholas among the refugees. The compass had pointed her directly to the Tranquility. Had she missed something? Had he been aboard one of the other airships anchored farther from the glacier? In all the excitement of the fire, the evacuation, and the explosion that had destroyed the ship, she had forgotten all about King Nicholas! What if he had been aboard the Tranquility and hadn't escaped? What if he had gone crashing thousands of feet into the valley below with the wreckage of the airship?

"No!" she said, closing her eyes tightly.

He threw his arms around her and hugged her. "It's all right, Elizabeth," he said.

"But I failed," she said, crying softly. "You don't understand. Carol trusted me to find her husband, and I thought I could. But I couldn't. The compass *said* he was here. But he isn't. And when I didn't see him, I just *forgot* about him."

"You didn't forget about him. You just didn't recognize him—which is perfectly understandable, since you've never met him before!"

Elizabeth stopped crying when she realized the little boy wasn't *talking* like a little boy.

She pulled back from his embrace and opened her eyes.

There, standing in front of her, was a full-grown man with a long white beard, dressed in a wool-and-velvet maroon coat and gloves very like her own. A matching hat that looked like a nightcap with a white ball on the end of it topped his head.

Elizabeth blinked: "Who are you?" she said, puzzled. "Where did the boy go?"

"You still don't recognize me, do you?" the man said. "As I said, it is understandable, since you've never met me!" He chuckled merrily: "Aha! A-ho-ho-ho!" Then he paused and said, "I *am* the boy."

"I don't understand," said Elizabeth, fumbling inside her coat and pulling out the Spectacles of Samwell Spink.

She was suddenly anxious. What if this was another one of Nigel's tricks?

"Go ahead," said the man. "We have time. Time, in fact, is all we have."

She scowled, then strapped the spectacles on and adjusted them to reveal his aura. It was gold and sparkly, just like Carol Kringle's.

"You're not Nigel," she said.

"No, I am most certainly *not* my brother." His tone was one of mere certainty and contained no hint of disdain.

"Your brother? That means..."

"King Nicholas, at your service." He bowed graciously.

Now, it was her turn to throw her arms around *him*. She ran up and embraced him tightly. "But how?"

He chuckled his distinctive chuckle once again. "No matter how old we get—and I am very, very old—there is still a child inside each one of us," he said. "And no matter how young we are, there is always a grownup soon to be. Time is an illusion that fools all of us, unless we know how to see past it with new eyes."

"Like the spectacles," said Elizabeth.

"Like that, yes, but not exactly. We already have the eyes we need to see the truth of things. We've just forgotten where they are." He tapped his chest.

"But why did you appear as a child?" she asked him.

"I was scared," he said simply. "Wouldn't you have been, in my place?"

She nodded.

"The same way you have been scared for as long as you can remember. That's why you've always appeared as a young girl. It is how you've always thought of yourself, so that's just how you've been. But look." He reached inside his coat and pulled out a small hand mirror.

"Why do you carry that around with you?" Elizabeth asked.

"I like to look my best when visiting strangers' homes, and I do that quite a lot. It wouldn't do to arrive all covered in ash and soot."

Elizabeth laughed. It was the first time she could remember having done so in a very, very, very long time. She took the mirror and opened it, peering into its face. There, staring back at her, was a woman of middle years with golden hair, salted by streaks of silver over a high forehead. As she smiled, a dimple formed in her left cheek, the same as it always had. But otherwise, the image in the mirror looked much different—much, much older—than she herself had always felt.

Elizabeth's laughter faded. "Who is that?" she asked.

"You, of course," King Nicholas answered. "It would seem you have found your courage. You are no longer the scared child you always thought you were."

Then, she remembered. She remembered living alone in Ridley Manor for many years after her parents died, slain on the road to York by a highwayman who was never caught. They had left her behind, in the care of her governess, while they had traveled to a Christmas Eve ball at a nearby estate. This, she now knew, was the true reason she never believed in Christmas. Her parents had left her behind, and had never returned. A stranger had arrived with news of their deaths, and she overheard him deliver the news to the governess as Elizabeth hid behind the door to the pantry. She had overheard everything, but she'd wanted to forget. In the end, she had wanted it so badly that she really did. She convinced herself that she'd never *had* any parents, because not having them was better than thinking they'd left her behind.

What they had left was enough money in their estate to pay for the governess to stay on at Ridley Manor and care for Elizabeth as long as she was needed. Her name was Miss Howell, but Elizabeth took to calling her Miss Owl as a form of endearment. Miss Owl had always made sure Elizabeth was fed, clothed, and cared for, over the course of many years. She's become the mother Elizabeth had forgotten she ever had.

Shortly after her parents died, Elizabeth remembered planting the labyrinth in their memory. She'd been barely eighteen at the time, and, after she'd planted it, she had refused to ever look at it again. It had been too painful. After a time, she'd made herself forget it was even there.

She'd made herself forget everything else, too, until all that remained was the little girl who had lived inside her before it all happened, staying alone inside that huge, dark mansion, with only Miss Howell for company. Most of the time, with just a single lamp lighting a single room by which she'd read and reread all the books her parents had kept in the manor's library.

There were stories there of gypsies and kobolds, of tree-men and knights and Greek heroes. There were spooky stories of All Hallows' Eve, and bright, cheery stories of Christmas, but she hadn't wanted to hear bright cheery stories after she'd learned of her parents' death. How could a world as cruel as this taunt children with tales of a kindly old man who gave good little children gifts on Christmas Eve? Such a man could not exist. Not in her world. Not in this world. If he did, she did not belong there.

"I don't belong here," said Elizabeth softly.

She realized why it had hurt her so much to hear that Carol had lost King Nicholas, that Dreqnir had been separated from his mother, and that Nicholas, when he had appeared as a child, seemed so alone.

It was because she had lost those she loved, too. It was because she, too, felt alone, though she had grown so accustomed to it that she almost had forgotten.

Nicholas hugged her tightly. "You *do* belong here, child. But this is not your time. And I fear that unless you find it, you will not solve the riddle of the labyrinth, and you will not find your true home."

Chapter Twenty

Labrys

Illian returned from exploring the tunnels to be sure that all of Nigel's men had gone. She had found no trace of them, but they had clearly departed in haste, she said, because they had left a large cache of weapons behind them. One of these she had retrieved to replace the spear that had been destroyed by Captain Prometheus' fireball. It was not, however, another spear, but rather, a handsome double-headed axe.

"A pelekys," Dreqnir said when he saw it. "The first great weapon of the Greeks."

"Or labrys," said Taradreq. "According to legend, the god Zeus used it to bring forth lightning by cleaving the heavens in two."

"Labrys," said Elizabeth. "It sounds like 'labyrinth.'"

"It comes from the same word," Taradreq said.

Elizabeth wondered if that meant anything. She thought it probably did, but she didn't know what. Just as interesting, she found, was the fact that no one seemed to be treating her any differently, now that she appeared as a grown woman rather than a young girl. It was as though everyone had seen her that way all along—everyone, that is, except she herself. She suspected they had probably seen King Nicholas that way, too, even though he had appeared as a young boy to her. That would explain why no one seemed to have been worried about failing to find him: They *had* found him, and they knew it. Elizabeth wondered what else she might be seeing differently than it really was.

Or hearing, for that matter. She was still hearing that faint music in her ears from somewhere far away, but no one else seemed to hear it. The tune changed from time to time, and sometimes it fell silent altogether. There were times when she recognized the music, and others when she did not. She mentioned it to the others, but they seemed less concerned about it than they were about returning home—Dreqnir and Taradreq to *Dragehjem*, and King Nicholas to his North Pole Village. Not only did he miss Carol, but Dreqnir had told him what had befallen his factory, and he was eager to return and oversee its reconstruction.

They were also concerned about something else: The evernight had still not ended, even though Lord Nigel had been defeated and the king had been rescued. They all wondered what it would take to end the unending darkness and bring the sun back to the vault of the sky. She remembered something Carol had said: that the village's high counselor was convinced that the one who possessed the Talismans of Time could restore the world to sunlight. She knew the spectacles and the pocketwatch were two of the talismans, and she had found two more—the compass and the map—at *Dragehjem.* That would mean she had four of the talismans, but she didn't know how many others there were, or whether all of them were needed in order to lift the curse.

Perhaps King Nicholas would know.

"Have you heard of the Talismans of Time?" she asked.

He nodded.

"How many are there, and where can I find them?"

Nicholas scratched his beard thoughtfully. "Well," he said, "you already have five of them."

"Five?"

"The pocketwatch, the map, the compass and the spectacles."

That was four.

"The fifth is the Pathfinder of Destiny."

Elizabeth's eyes widened. "The axe!"

Illian fingered the weapon. "Are you saying *this* is the Pathfinder of Destiny?"

"Well...," said Nicholas.

Illiana stepped forward and offered the axe to Elizabeth. "If you are meant to use these talismans of which you speak, you should carry all of them."

But Elizabeth declined. "You should hold it for now," she said. "I think you are better equipped to use it than I."

Illiana nodded and stood at attention: "I will wield it only in your service. You have my word."

Elizabeth looked down, feeling embarrassed. Part of her wanted to object; she didn't feel qualified to have anyone serve her, even less so having seen the plight of the slaves aboard the Tranquility. She even felt guilty, now that she thought about it, at having allowed Miss Howell to look after her so completely all those years. But when she looked back up into Illian's eyes, she saw not the shame of servitude, but the commitment of one who took pride in offering service. That was different, she supposed, and so she said, simply, "Thank you."

Then, she turned back to Nicholas. "How many other talismans are there?"

"Two," he said.

"Where are they? Can we use the compass and the map to find them?"

But Nicholas looked down, a troubled expression on his face. "They are not here," he said simply.

"Yes, but can we get to them?" said Taradreq. "Our wings are at your disposal."

Dreqnir nodded in agreement.

"I fear you cannot help us, dragon friends," said Nicholas. "When I said they are not here, I meant they are not here *anywhere*. They do not exist in this time. The Flute of Pan's Third Daughter was cast into the River of Time and is locked inside the labyrinth of Daedalus, a place outside of time. The other is the Wild Card, a keepsake that depicts a baseball player who will not be born until the next century."

"What is baseball?" asked Elizabeth.

"They play it in America," said Dreqnir. "It's a little like cricket."

"Boring," said Elizabeth, and the dragons both laughed. But she was thinking about something else. They had mentioned a labyrinth, and *she* was in a labyrinth. Or, at least, she had entered one. What if her labyrinth and the labyrinth of Daedalus were one and the same? She thought of the talismans. Each of them had served her at a particular time. Without the map and compass, she could not have found Nigel, and without the pocketwatch, she could not have defeated him. Without the spectacles, she would not have known whom to trust. The only talisman she hadn't used so far was the one she'd just discovered: the labrys. The Pathfinder of Destiny. Why should an axe be called a pathfinder, she wondered?

"This pathfinder. How is it used?"

"If Zeus used it to cleave the heavens in two and create light, maybe we're supposed to do the same thing," Illiana said. "If one of the dragons can take me close enough to the sky, maybe I can use it to rip the veil of darkness in two and let the sun back in."

"I don't think the sun works that way," said Elizabeth. "I don't think there's an actual veil in the sky that can be torn in two."

"Oh," said Illiana, disappointed. "It would have been fun."

"Yes, it would have," said Dreqnir. "But she's right. The story is a myth, and myths tend to deal in symbols, not actual things."

"Dragons are supposed to be myths, too," Illiana protested.

Dreqnir said nothing. She had a point.

Each of the other talismans had given her some idea of how they should be used, but she didn't get any sense of that from the labrys. Instead, she kept getting distracted by the music that had started playing in her head again.

This time, it was a song she knew well. It had been playing on the gramophone, a device her parents had bought a few years earlier, on the night she learned of their deaths.

An old folk tune, it went like this:

Tell me the tales that to me were so dear,
Long, long ago, long, long ago,
Sing me the songs I delighted to hear,
Long, long ago, long ago,
Now you are come all my grief is removed,
Let me forget that so long you have roved.
Let me believe that you love as you loved,
Long, long ago, long ago.

Do you remember the paths where we met?
Long, long ago, long, long ago.
Ah, yes, you told me you'd never forget,
Long, long ago, long ago.
Then to all others, my smile you preferred,
Love, when you spoke, gave a charm to each word.
Still my heart treasures the phrases I heard,
Long, long ago, long ago.

Tho' by your kindness my fond hopes were raised,
Long, long ago, long, long ago.
You by more eloquent lips have been praised,
Long, long ago, long, long ago,
But, by long absence your truth has been tried,

Still to your accents I listen with pride,
Blessed as I was when I sat by your side.
Long, long ago, long ago.

It made her think of her parents, and how they'd left her: the thing she'd never wanted to think of again.

The others were all staring at her.

"What's wrong?" asked Illian.

Elizabeth couldn't speak. She had felt all the blood drain from her face, and still the tune kept playing in her ears.

"Make it stop," she said finally, desperate. "Please, dear God, make it stop." She started crying.

"Make what stop?" Taradreq asked in confusion.

"Don't you hear it? That music. It's coming from... it's coming from over there!" She pointed to the end of the tunnel where they were standing, at an oddly placed wooden closet, like a wardrobe or armoire. She didn't remember seeing it there before, and evidently, none of the others did, either.

"Where did that come from?" asked Illian.

"I didn't see it there before," said Dreqnir.

But Elizabeth didn't care about that. All she cared about was the music, which seemed to be getting louder, even if no one else could hear it.

"MAKE IT STOP!" she shouted.

But nobody moved.

Her mind was racing, in a frenzy. She only knew she had to stop the music from playing. She couldn't wait any longer, or it would drive her mad.

In an instant, she lunged at Illian and grabbed the labrys away from her. The spearmaiden was taken so completely off her guard that she released it before she realized what was happening.

Wrapping both hands tight around the handle, Elizabeth sprinted toward the armoire, tears streaming from her eyes as they narrowed and focused on the object of her fury. As she ran, the music seemed to grow louder. It sounded like it was being played on a flute. How could the others not have heard it?

She didn't stop to think about what King Nicholas had said: that a flute was one of the two missing talismans.

She just knew that she...

Had.

To.

Make.

It.

Stop.

She was nearly upon it now. She raised the axe above her head and brought it down with a vengeance on the closet, sending wooden shards and splinters flying. She stopped and planted her feet and squared her shoulders. She lifted the axe above her head and brought it down again. And again. And again. Until the doors to the armoire were shattered and ruined, with almost nothing left attached to the hinges.

She stopped, breathing hard, and stared.

What lay beyond was more than a clothes closet. A whole lot more.

Chapter Twenty-One

Timeswitch

Isis jumped and yowled, and Ruffus began barking excitedly. Alex dropped the flute, as something came crashing through the wall that had seemed solid and impregnable just a moment ago.

Isis leapt onto the boy's shoulder, her nine tails twirling like rotors on a helicopter. They lifted her into the air, and she lunged, claws extended and flaying the empty air. The cat literally flew toward the breach in the wall, which had been created by the two-headed axe wielded by the woman who stood there.

"Alamina?"

Alex was dumbfounded. "Isis, stop!"

The cat's tail stopped spinning, and she dropped to

the ground with as much grace as possible, landing (of course) on all four paws.

She immediately started grooming herself.

"Alamina?" Alex repeated.

"I... don't... know that name," Elizabeth said, trying to catch her breath after all that exertion. "Who are you?"

"I'm Alex," said the boy. "Don't you remember me?"

Elizabeth stood up straighter. "My name is Elizabeth," she said. The music had stopped, and she was regaining her wits. She didn't recognize the boy in front of her at all, and she didn't recognize the name Alamina, either. He had obviously confused her with someone else.

"I'm sorry," she said. "I don't know you. ... Where are we?"

"At the center of the maze or the labyrinth or whatever it is," said Alex, watching as a second woman stepped through the gap behind Alamina, who for some reason was calling herself Elizabeth. She wore an expression of fierce determination that seemed to be a regular part of her facial features.

Behind her, two huge dragons pushed their way through, tearing down pieces of the wall around the edges of the opening to make it large enough for them to pass through. And after them, a man with a long white beard and ample belly made his entrance—a man who looked for all the world like... Santa Claus. He strode over to a big wooden chair and sat his ample bottom on its seat.

"Ah, much better," he declared, exhaling contentedly.

Ruffus trotted up to the bearded man and started sniffing at his feet. The man, in turn, smiled and reached down to scratch behind the bloodhound's ears.

Alex felt as though he had stumbled into a costume party.

Well, it *was* Halloween.

Isis's eyes brightened. "Hello, Chris," she said, padding across the floor and jumping into his lap. He rewarded her by rubbing her back just in front of her tails, and she responded with a contented purr.

"Hello, old friend," he said. "And thank you for not calling me 'King Nicholas.' Living up to formal names and ceremonial titles can get exhausting after a while!"

Alex wondered briefly how the cat knew the old man, He did not, however, consider the possibility that the man might really *be* Santa Claus, and that Santa Claus traveled extensively for his job—which meant he likely met any number of cats, dogs, parakeets, hamsters and goldfish in children's homes around the world.

He did not consider these things, because he wasn't focused on the bearded man. His eyes kept being drawn back to the woman who was calling herself Elizabeth—but whose true name, he was sure, was Alamina.

Her eyes, likewise, were fixed on him.

"I *do* know you," she said at last. "Or, at least, I feel I should."

Then, suddenly, a realization dawned on Alex. He didn't know where it had come from—perhaps from some other time entirely—but he suddenly knew who the woman standing in front of him was. Or had been. Or, perhaps, both.

"You're her," he said simply. "You're the girl I sent the map and compass to."

The girl reached inside her coat and pulled out the two talismans. "These?"

"Yes," he said. "Likho sent them to you, magically."

"That explains how they just 'appeared' in our treasury," said Dreqnir. "Karanadreq will be relieved to know she did not make a mistake with the inventory."

Taradreq laughed at this, but neither Alex nor Elizabeth was paying attention to the dragons. Elizabeth didn't know who 'Likho' was, but she did know that she couldn't have come this far without the map and, especially, the compass. "Thank you," she said, although it seemed far too small a thing to say, considering what the boy had done.

Nicholas looked up from petting Isis and addressed Alex: "Am I correct in concluding that you have the other two talismans: the flute"—he motioned toward the instrument, which still lay on the floor where Alex had dropped it—"and the Wild Card"?

Alex nodded, pulling the Lou Gehrig baseball card out of his pocket.

"Then we have all we need," he declared, standing.

"For what?"

"To banish the evernight and return to the realm of time."

Alex looked puzzled. "What do you mean, 'return'?"

"Just as I said," Nicholas declared. "We are at the center of the labyrinth, which is, by its nature, a place out of time. That is why it's so difficult to escape from this place. Only the one who holds all six talismans can do it."

Elizabeth turned to him. "Six? I thought there were seven." She ticked them off on her fingers: "The pocketwatch... the compass... the map... the spectacles... the flute... the wild card... and the axe."

Nicholas shook his head. "Well, there *are* technically seven talismans, but the axe is not among them."

Elizabeth frowned. "But the Pathfinder of Destiny. You said..."

"You *assumed*," Nicholas corrected her, a twinkle in his eye. "The axe is not the Pathfinder of Destiny. *You* are."

"I don't understand."

"Oh, don't get me wrong," he said. "The labrys is, indeed, a magical tool, but only in the hands of the proper person. I was a little worried when you allowed Illian to keep it in her care. She could not have breached the walls that barred us from the heart of the labyrinth. Only a Time Wielder could have done that. Only the Pathfinder of Destiny." He pointed at her to emphasize his point. "You."

"This is all very interesting, Alamina," said Alex.

"Elizabeth," she corrected.

He ignored it. "But now that you're here," he said, "we still need to find our way home."

"And before you can do that," Nicholas said. "You have to know where 'home' is."

Alex opened his mouth and was about to say, "Iowa." But then he remembered he had never felt at home there. He had come all this way, he realized, and he still didn't know where home really was.

"I know where home is," said Elizabeth. "It's Ridley Manor, my home in Yorkshire."

Nicholas smiled and nodded. "Yes, it is. And there's your answer." He was smiling not at Elizabeth, but at Alex.

"I don't understand," he said.

Nicholas scratched his beard. "How can I explain this?" he said, pausing and frowning as he cast his gaze upward. "You came here for a reason," he said at last. "To find your way home."

Alex nodded. He remembered again what Likho had said: that the entire world depended on him finding his way home. But why?

"Your home is not where—or, more importantly, *when* —you thought it should be," Nicholas continued. "You see, you and Elizabeth were both living in the wrong time. Each of you was supposed to be in the timespace occupied by the other, and because of this mix-up, the entire world has been thrown off-kilter, so to speak."

"A knot in the timeline?" said Taradreq.

"Not exactly," Nicholas answered. He plucked a thread from his coat and held each end between a thumb and forefinger.

"It's natural to think that time runs in a line, from one set endpoint to another," he explained. "But that is not how it works. If the truth be told, time runs in a circle, and the world's very existence relies upon that circle remaining whole. If it is broken at any point, it ceases to function; like a broken gear on a bicycle." He looked at Alex. "Like the one I brought you for Christmas four years ago."

Alex's mouth dropped open.

Nicholas went on: "If the gear on a bicycle breaks, the chain will come loose, and you won't be able to get anywhere at all."

"So. time runs in a circle? Like the face of a clock?" said Elizabeth.

"Sort of," said Nicholas. "As long as it's not digital." He winked at Alex. Elizabeth, being from the nineteenth century, looked clueless. "You can jump on or off at any point on the circle—if you know what you are doing. You just can't break the circle, or there will be nowhere left to go. Time will literally collapse in on itself, and everything will cease to exist. That's what very nearly happened."

"But why?" asked Alex.

"Because somehow, you and Elizabeth switched times. For most people, this wouldn't matter. But for you two, it's different. One of you is a Time Wielder, and the other a Memory Master. Your gifts are exceedingly rare. Indeed, one would be hard-pressed to find two more gifted individuals in the entire annals of history. If you don't switch back, things that need to be accomplished never will be—things upon which the fate of the world depends. It will break the wheel."

Elizabeth stared at him. "So, that's why we're here? To switch back?"

Nicholas nodded. "That's why you both had to come here. The center of the labyrinth is a place out of time. It's a crossroads where all times meet and no time exists. From here, you can step out into *any* time you wish—if you can get out."

Alex nodded toward the Minute-Hour, who seemed to be coming out of his stupor. "He has been stuck here for... I don't know how long."

"Neither do I," Nicholas admitted. "Time loses its

meaning here, so it's impossible to know."

Asterion's eyelids flickered open, and he got slowly to his feet, rubbing his eyes and looking around him. He looked at the dragons, at the spearmaiden, and at Nicholas. But before he could say anything, his gaze settled on the hole at the far end of the room—the hole through which Elizabeth and the others had come. When he saw it, his mouth fell open and his eyes grew wide. He clenched both fists and sprang forward, racing at full speed toward the aperture.

"I'm free! I'm free!" he shouted as he leapt into the void.

Then his voice cut off, and he was gone.

"Where did he go?" asked Alex.

"A glacier in Scandinavia," Illian said matter-of-factly. "He'll wish he had dressed a little warmer."

But Nicholas was shaking his head. "It doesn't work like that," he said. "There's no telling where he is now. When you leave the center of the labyrinth, you might end up anywhere at any time. Unless you set your destination before you leave, you're just as likely to end up in Madrid during the Spanish Inquisition or in sub-Saharan Africa during the age of the dinosaurs. There's no telling."

"Oh, dear," said Elizabeth.

But Alex was far less concerned about the bull-headed man than he was about how to get home—even if home wasn't where he'd thought it would be.

"How do we set our destination?" asked Alex. "Do we click our heels together and say, 'There's no place like home'?"

Elizabeth looked at him, baffled.

"It was a joke," he said.

Nicholas looked at Elizabeth. "You are a Time Wielder and the Pathfinder of Destiny. As such, you simply need to focus on the path before you, the way you did when you brought us all here."

He turned to Alex. "Your task is a little less direct, but well within your means to accomplish. Because of your gift, you have it within yourself to travel to anyplace for which you have a memory."

Alex frowned. "That would be fine," he said. "Except, if I'm supposed to switch places with Alamina... er... Elizabeth, and I have no memory of Yorkshire. I've never been outside of Iowa!"

Nicholas smiled. "You are a Memory Master, and because of this, you can gain access to any other person's memory that they agree to share. I believe Elizabeth would consent to share hers."

"Of course," she said.

"Then all you have to do is recall the memory you wish to share, and send it to Alex through your mind's eye."

Illian spoke up: "What about the rest of us? Will we

be stuck here?"

Nicholas waved a hand reassuringly. "Not at all," he said. "But you will have to choose between accompanying one or the other of your friends. You will need to find new lives in new times and new places, but I'm quite sure all of you are up to the challenge."

Dreqnir looked distressed. "But what will happen to *Dragehjem* without a queen?"

"I'm sure Karanadreq is more than up to the task," Taradreq replied.

"I've never had a home, except in Nigel's service," said Illian. "Anything else will be a welcome change."

In the end, they all chose to stay with the person they'd come with: the dragons and Illian with Elizabeth; Ruffus and Isis with Alex. As to King Nicholas, he chose to go with Alex, explaining—quite reasonably—that it made the most sense for him to return at an earlier time, so as not to miss out on any Christmases.

Elizabeth found a piece of paper and spent several moments writing something on it. Then she gladly shared her memories with Alex, and the two of them, so closely bound together by destiny but only recently united, made ready to part ways.

"Where will I end up?" she asked him. "What can I expect?"

He told her about television and video games and compact discs and VCRs. He told her about "Back to the

Future" and "Bill and Ted's Excellent Adventure"; about Iowa and the corn maze that had brought him here. "A lot has changed in 1991," he said.

She chuckled. "I'm sure it has. Or will."

She laughed again, and then they both grew somber. The boy stepped close to her and threw his arms around her.

"I guess we won't see each other again after this," he said. "A century is a long ways apart."

"You never know," she said, hugging him back. "I am a Time Wielder, after all." She laughed. She didn't even really know what that meant.

Before they parted, she slipped the note she had written into his hand. "Give this to Miss Owl," she said. "It will let her know that I'm all right, and that I want her to take care of you."

He took the note and put it in his pocket, next to the Lou Gehrig baseball card, patting it twice to be sure it was secure.

Then he smiled, and let her go, and turned toward the aperture. Waving goodbye to the dragons and Illian, he ran toward it and leapt through—in precisely the right way to come out at the entrance to the labyrinth in the back of Ridley Manor just before the turn of the twentieth century. Then Elizabeth, in her turn, jumped through the breach she had created and found herself in a cornfield in rural Iowa on a Halloween morning.

Yes, morning.

Daylight had returned, and the evernight had ended. The same was true in the Yorkshire of Alex's new-old time, although the sun was hidden behind a blanket of fog.

King Nicholas found his sleigh waiting for him on the roof of the manor, and Carol was there to greet him with a tight and very relieved embrace. It was Christmas Day, she told him, and he had missed his customary rounds. But the Alfur had managed to rebuild the factory, and she had taken the reins to deliver every single one of his toys in the good king's absence.

Cary looked over his shoulder, nodded and snorted a "hello."

"Good to see you again, old friend," he said. "I think it's about time we head home."

Chapter Twenty-Two

Homecomings

Miss Howell was surprised to see the boy standing at the door to Ridley Manor.

"May I help you, young man?" she asked. Her gaze moved briefly to the bloodhound seated beside him and the odd-looking cat—with nine tails! —weaving her way between his legs and circling around him, purring.

"Hello," said Isis.

"Hello," said Ruffus.

"Hello," said Alex.

Then he reached into his pocket, and a look of panic crossed his face. He found the note Elizabeth had given him, but the baseball card was gone!

"What's wrong?" Miss Owl asked in a hooey-hoo

voice.

Alex looked puzzled but just shook his head. Maybe the card *couldn't* come with him, because Lou Gehrig hadn't been born yet. Of course, *he*—Alex—hadn't been born yet, and that hadn't stopped him, but this mystery was one for another time—and one he certainly didn't want to share with the woman in front of him. He was here, in this time and place, all by himself, and he didn't want to alienate his only potential friend by telling her some unbelievable story about being from the future.

As it turned out, though, Elizabeth's note told her exactly that:

Dearest Miss Owl,

I'm so thankful for everything you've done for me, and I'm sorry for being so difficult to get on with. I'm afraid I never got over my parents' passing, and I left you to deal with everything that went with that. I realize now how terribly unfair that was, and how unfair it is to ask you what I'm about to ask.

You may find this unbelievable, and I scarcely believe it myself, but I wasn't supposed to be living there with you. I'm not sure how, but I was living in the wrong time, and I've been able to return to my proper place in history. At least, I hope so. This must sound like madness, and I don't blame you if you laugh out loud at how preposterous it all sounds, but I can assure you I'm not making it up. Something tells me that you'll take me at my word, but even if you don't, I still have a momentous favor I must ask.

The boy with whom I sent this note is named Alex, and he is the one who was supposed to have been living in your time. Sending him back there, I'm told, will set things right, but he's just a child still and all alone in the world. If you would be so kind as to look after him, as you looked after me, I would be forever grateful (whatever "forever" might mean in a world of twisted time!). Teach him what you taught me, and learn from him, as well. I have a feeling he will have a lot of things to share as he grows older. It's just a feeling, yes, but feelings are something I'm learning to trust.

Give him everything you would have given to me. My parents had so many dreams for me, and I set them aside because of my grief at their passing. Perhaps, however, some good may still come of their intentions. Perhaps young Alex can make use of their generosity in ways I never could.

I'm afraid the chances of us ever seeing each other again are remote, at best. My new home is so far in the future that our paths are unlikely to cross again. Please know that I have loved you like my own mother, and that I still do! Take good care of Alex, and of yourself. I know you will because you always did with me.

Eternally,
Elizabeth

Miss Howell read the letter, then folded it up and put it in her coat pocket. Alex regretted not having read it; it hadn't seemed right to do so when Elizabeth had given it to him, but now he was very curious indeed.

Miss Howell, however, did not seem inclined to indulge his curiosity.

"Very good," she said. "Now come with me."

She escorted him into Ridley Manor, which, from that day forward, became his new home. Miss Owl took him under her proverbial wing, and looked after him until he came of age. He read all the books Elizabeth had read in the extensive library at Ridley Manor. Not only did he read them, he memorized them, the same way he had memorized the back of every baseball card he'd ever owned.

This, he supposed, was that talent that made him what King Nicholas had called a Memory Master.

Miss Owl, on the other hand, had a different gift. Alex learned, not too long after arriving, that her name really *was* Miss Owl—and with good reason: She was a Shape Changer, whose particular skill enabled her to take on many different forms. Her favorite of these just happened to be the long-eared owl from whom she took her name.

He also learned that Elizabeth's parents had been extremely wealthy, which came as no real surprise considering the size of Ridley Manor. They had left a trust significantly larger than what was needed to cover the cost of Miss Owl's services. They had intended to fund Elizabeth's education when she came of age, and to support whatever adventures she might decide to undertake in adulthood.

But Elizabeth had chosen to remain at the manor, and most of the funds her parents had left for her had remained unused.

Miss Owl shared these facts with Alex when he came of age and it became clear that Elizabeth herself would not be returning. She sat down beside him and, producing the letter Elizabeth had left for him, finally allowed him to read it. She pointed, in particular, to the words "Give him everything you would have given to me."

"Elizabeth was left with a significant inheritance," she said. "But she is not here, and she wished it to pass to you. It is up to you to decide what to do with it."

Her words took Alex by surprise. He had not considered that he might come into such a windfall, and his first thought was to go out and buy all the baseball cards in the world. Then he remembered that there were no baseball cards in Yorkshire, and such collectibles were only just now starting to be produced in America. The first sports cards came in packages of cigarettes and loose tobacco, and Alex had no particular love for tobacco.

Then he remembered his other dream, the one he had all but forgotten since he had come to Yorkshire.

A school.

The school he had attended in Moravia had never

seemed quite right to him. The subjects seemed irrelevant, the teachers ill-equipped to teach students with unusual gifts, and the campus itself. ... Well, it wasn't as though there was anything wrong with it; it was a perfectly adequate facility, with desks and chalkboards, a playground and a cafeteria. But it still *felt* wrong to Alex.

He remembered that feeling as he thought about it, and he realized that he had an entirely different feeling about where he was now. Ridley Manor, with its vast library of books, had become more of a school to him than his old elementary school in Iowa had ever been. It had no desks, no chalkboard, no playground and no cafeteria. But none of that mattered. It *felt* right. And it was such a vast estate that it was big enough to actually *be* a school.

It would only take a little bit of work.

"What if...?" he began.

And Miss Owl smiled as he described his dream of a school for gifted youth, a dream that now took clearer form in his mind's eye.

What if there were a place for children with talents such as he and Elizabeth—and Miss Owl herself—possessed? He saw, in his mind's eye, old bedrooms converted into rooms for instruction; the great central room as an assembly hall; the grounds being used for exercise; the kitchens, large enough to serve hundreds during a seasonal ball, serving the pupils at a grand country school. The labyrinth itself could be the ultimate classroom, where students could hone and master the skills they had been given, where they could carry on the work that had been entrusted to Elizabeth and Alex.

The world had been in peril once. What if it were again?

"I think it's a wonderful idea," said Miss Owl.

"We could call it the Academy of the Labyrinth," Alex said, as he walked over to the window overlooking the manor gardens.

To his amazement, the labyrinth was gone.

He turned around, a shocked and slightly panicked expression on his face. "What happened to it?" he said.

Miss Owl came over and stood beside him, looking down on the fountains and flowerbeds below them.

"I think it only appears when a Pathfinder has need of it," Miss Owl said.

A Pathfinder. "King Nicholas called Elizabeth the Pathfinder of Destiny."

Miss Owl nodded. "And it appeared to her when she needed it. I trust it will appear when you need it to, as well. There are four great gifts: the gifts of the Time Wielder, the Memory Master, the Shape Changer, and the Dream Strider. A Pathfinder can possess any one of these gifts. Or more than one. Or all of them. It is entirely possible that you are a Pathfinder, as well. Indeed, I consider it highly likely. The labyrinth, I think, will reappear when you most need it."

Alex forced a smile but still looked worried. "Then perhaps," he said at last, "we should call it the Academy of the Lost Labyrinth."

Miss Owl nodded. "At least until it is found again."

Elizabeth looked around her. Something felt wrong.

"I don't think we're where we are supposed to be," she said.

"I wouldn't know," said Illian. "I've never been here before."

The two dragons flapped their wings to cushion their landing as they descended from the sky. Their massive feet crushed corn stalks beneath their weight as they landed, creating giant footprints.

"Wasn't there supposed to be a corn maze here?" said Elizabeth.

"I heard him say so, yes," said Dreqnir.

"I see corn, but no maze," said Taradreq. "I didn't see anything that looked like one from overhead, either."

Elizabeth felt uneasy and unsure of herself. King Nicholas had sounded so sure of things when he'd pronounced her the Pathfinder of Destiny; when he had told her that she simply needed to focus on the path before her, and she would get where she needed to go. She wished she were as sure of herself. She had never done anything like this before. What if she'd gotten it wrong? Something told her she *had* gotten it wrong. There should have been a maze here, but there wasn't.

"It looks like what Alex described as the place he was from," said Illian. "Iowa, he called it."

Elizabeth nodded, then it hit her: What if the place were right, but the time was wrong? She turned around and looked behind her. They were near a hard-surface road, and across that road stood a building with a sign beside it. Maybe someone in that building could tell them.

She beckoned the others with a wave of her hand, and they followed her as she started to cross the road, then jumped back as a metal carriage—moving without the benefit of any horses and much faster than any horses could travel—whizzed past. Other, similar metal carriages followed, some moving in the same direction and others the opposite way along the road. One of the drivers turned to look at them and, upon seeing the two dragons standing there, steered his car off the road and into the cornfield. It stalled there, and streams of white smoke rose from the front end of it.

The driver got out and ran away.

The sound of the crash must have been heard inside the building across the road, because several people came out the front door and looked to see what was happening. When they saw the dragons, they all jumped in metal chariots of their own, which made a whirring-wheezing noise before their wheels started turning and they departed, all in a very big hurry.

Taradreq raised an eyebrow. "Some things haven't changed."

Dreqnir sighed. "Some things never do."

When there were no more metal carriages to contend with, Elizabeth and the others crossed the road toward the building. They got there to find it deserted; not one soul had been brave enough to stick around with two dragons approaching. Looking in the window, they saw rows of colorful packages, and windowed cases, in the back, filled with bottles and cans. A few circular seats, without backs, lined a counter to one side, upon which sat a couple of plain-looking plates with half-eaten sandwiches and cups for tea or coffee.

"What is this place?" asked Illian.

Elizabeth shook her head and turned her attention to a metal box with a clear window in front, anchored to the ground beside the door. Inside the box were sheaves of folded papers with writing in large letters at the top: "The Moravia Union."

And there was also, in smaller letters, a date: "Monday, November 1, 1971"

"Alex said he was from 1991," she said. "If this date is correct, we're twenty years too early."

Chapter Twenty-Three

Closing the Circle

Elizabeth spent those next twenty years waiting for the chance to correct her mistake. She traveled back to Yorkshire, where she was astonished to find that Alex had transformed her former home into an academy for gifted students. Then he simply vanished, leaving her in charge. His disappearance seemed to confirm her worst fears: that she had made a horrible mistake by arriving in the future too early, and that this mistake had undone everything.

It also left her feeling very much alone.

The dragons returned to *Dragehjem*, but Dreqnir found himself restless. Much had changed since his last, brief sojourn there, and he had been away so long already—when he was bonded to Tar Kidron—that it scarcely felt like home to him. After a brief visit to the dragons' mountain home in Scandinavia, he flew back to the Academy, where he became the first instructor Elizabeth hired during her tenure. His initial task then was to enroll in one of the courses himself: Changing Shapes and Changing Back. It simply would not do to attract attention to the academy by having a dragon in residence there. Elizabeth could only imagine what might happen if a traveling salesman or curious passer-by caught sight of him.

Dreqnir had to take the course remotely from a barn on the property that was converted into a residence, because he didn't fit in the classroom, let alone behind one of the desks. Fortunately, he turned out to have an aptitude for shape-changing (magical creatures being more naturally attuned to the gifts than humans are). He initially resisted taking human form, but warmed to the idea when Elizabeth suggested he could create a new persona of his own choice. He threw himself into the project then, scouring a number of movie videos before settling on a form that looked quite similar to Conan the Barbarian. Elizabeth insisted he exchange the leather crown and bare torso for a proper suit and tie, to which he—reluctantly—agreed.

Taradreq did not return with him. She stayed on at *Dragehjem*, taking the new title of Dragon Queen Mother and advising her successor, Karanadreq. (Dragons, it should be noted, are known for their longevity and can live for hundreds of years. Although Taradreq was still fairly young by the standards of her kind, she thought it improper to unseat Karanadreq from the throne, particularly since she seemed to be such a capable queen.)

Having Dreqnir on the faculty helped Elizabeth feel a little more comfortable in her new role. It was good to have a friend there, especially since Miss Owl was no longer with her. The Shape Changer has passed many years ago, Elizabeth learned. She had depended on the kindly governess to care for her ever since her parents' deaths; now she was left to depend on herself—and care for the hundreds of students enrolled at the Academy, as well. It felt overwhelming, taking on such a heavy burden. More than once, she wished Alex had been able to remain at the Academy long enough to offer some guidance, but she held herself responsible for his disappearance. If she had appeared at the proper point in the future, he would not have vanished.

At least, that's what she believed.

It felt no less overwhelming after twenty years had passed, even though she became more accustomed to her role. Some things had changed: She called herself Alamina now, and she had earned the trust and respect of her students. But others had not: She felt no more confident in her ability to time jump than she had after it all went wrong—when she left the labyrinth.

And she dreaded having to go back in.

When she emerged from the labyrinth for a second time, the first thing Alamina did was look around her.

She breathed a sigh of relief to find the Academy was still there. The words "Ridley Institute" were still plainly visible over the front entrance, and students were still hurrying across the grounds to reach their next classes before the second passing bell sounded.

But she had to be sure.

She waved down Dreqnir, who was striding purposely across the lawn—in his Conan form—toward his next assignment.

He stopped at the sound of her voice and jogged up to the place where she was standing, the three Romani boys and a few other students dressed in traditional Roma attire standing behind her.

"Where have you been?" he asked. "We've been worried. The labyrinth appeared and you disappeared. So did some of the students. But I see they're all accounted for, as well." He nodded toward the students behind her.

"A field trip," Alamina said. "To show the brothers where they came from. Although at least one of them got himself in serious trouble." She glared at Django, who shrugged and smiled sheepishly. "He was so proud that he had studied all about Likho before we left, but apparently, he didn't study enough. He almost ruined everything by telling Alex not to give the map and compass to the girl. To me, that is. And after that, he nearly didn't make it out of the labyrinth."

"Who's Likho?" Dreqnir asked.

"Someone nearly as scary as you!" Alamina said. She was trying to lighten the mood, more to ease her own anxiety than anything else.

It didn't work.

"Dreqnir, what day is it?" she asked.

"Friday."

"The date. I mean the date."

"November 1, 1991."

"You're sure." She held her breath.

"I'm sure."

Alamina allowed herself to exhale. This time, she had emerged from the labyrinth on the proper date. Perhaps she had made the most of that precious commodity so many never get: a second chance.

Just then, Mrs. Lightjacket came running up to them. A tall, slender woman with ghost-white hair, sunken cheeks, and dazzling blue eyes, she was among the most senior faculty members, having begun her tenure a decade before Alamina's arrival. She was, by the time she reached them, decidedly out of breath—and clearly flustered. This was very much out of character for the woman, who had a reputation among the students for keeping her cool no matter what. Her ability to do so had even earned her the nickname "The Unflappable Mrs. Lightjacket."

"Headmistress… I'm… sorry to… interrupt," she panted. "But… there's someone… to see you… in your office."

"Who is it, Emily?" Alamina said.

"I think you'd better come and see. You too, professor Dreqnir."

Alamina dismissed the three Romani boys and the others who had accompanied her into the labyrinth, and followed Mrs. Lightjacket, who, despite being winded, had started running again, back toward the school entrance.

"Who on earth could have affected her so?" Alamina asked.

Dreqnir just shook his head, jogging beside her.

When they reached Alamina's office, she opened the door and saw who it was with her own eyes. But she had to blink twice and rub them to make sure they weren't playing tricks on her.

"Headmaster?"

"Good grief, Elizabeth. After all this time, you can certainly call me Alex."

"Nobody calls me Elizabeth anymore."

"Of course!" he said. "A rose by any name..." He started to bow and nearly lost his balance, catching himself by placing a hand on Alamina's desk.

She smiled and stared at the man in front of her, who looked exactly the way he had twenty years ago, when last she'd seen him. But how had he gotten here? Had he returned because she had succeeded in her mission? But no, that seemed impossible. He had been ninety-five years old then. Could he possibly have lived to be a hundred and fifteen?

"How...?"

"Don't worry, Elizabeth. I don't want my old job back," he chuckled, leaning on his cane.

Having said that, he moved around her desk and sat in her chair. "Just allow an old man to sit in his old chair one last time. It *is* the most comfortable seat in the room."

"So it is." She sat down opposite him, and Dreqnir took a seat beside her.

"Who's your friend?" Alex asked, nodding toward Dreqnir.

"Oh, do you like the new look?" Dreqnir said, puffing his chest out. "I guess my Shape Changing prowess has fooled even you!"

"Dreqnir!" Alex said, pounding his cane once on the ground. "I recognize the voice. Good to see you, my friend. Is your mother here, too? And what of Illian?"

"Mother returned to *Dragehjem*," said Dreqnir.

"And Illian is our chief of security," Alamina added.

"Interesting," said Alex. "I never thought we'd need one of those."

"Some things have changed since you disappeared," she said. "More people have come nosing around, and I worried that unless I undid the damage I had done by going back into the labyrinth, something really bad might happen. Other things started fading, the same way you did. But I must have undone it—the damage, I mean—because the school is still here. And now you are, too! Although I have no idea how you managed to live as long as you have."

"About that...," Alex began awkwardly.

Alamina looked at him, waiting for him to continue.

"Well, I actually didn't *vanish* back then. Not exactly."

"Then what happened?"

She waited for an answer, and then it dawned on her. "You jumped!"

A broad smile formed on Alex's face. "I wasn't exactly thrilled about disappearing into nothing," he said, "so I took matters into my own hands."

"But I thought a Memory Master could only jump backward?"

Alex chuckled. "Normally, that would be true," he said. "But you forget, I'm originally *from* 1991, and I remember it quite well. It's an odd loophole, but forward is backward to me!"

Alamina shook her head. It made sense. But she was also embarrassed that she, a Time Wielder, had been too scared to try to jump again herself.

Alex must have seen that embarrassment in her face. "There's something I should tell you," he said. "You didn't do anything wrong."

Alamina raised her eyebrows. "What do you mean?"

"I mean, you were *supposed* to arrive twenty years ago," he said.

"That's impossible."

"It's not only possible, it's true. I'm sure you remember the second principle of temporal management."

Of course, she had it memorized. She recited it aloud: "In order change time, you must alter your perception of it."

"And its corollary?"

"Time is always as it should be."

"They call that the Principle of Destiny," Alex said. "And you, after all, are the *Pathfinder* of Destiny. It was, and is, impossible for you to do anything 'wrong' when it comes to time."

Alamina frowned.

"Think about it," Alex said. "If you hadn't jumped here twenty years before you thought you should have, you never would have met Ethelinda, and she never would have entrusted you with the Compass of the Seventh Kingdom."

Recognition dawned on Alamina's face. "And I never would have taken it into the labyrinth."

"And we both would have been stuck in there forever."

"And you would never have founded the Academy, which explains why everything was starting to fade away."

Alex nodded. "It's hard to believe I was a young boy just yesterday on the calendar, and today, I'm an old man."

"I suppose that's the way it feels for all of us," said Alamina. "Just not literally so!"

Alex laughed.

"Do you ever wonder what happened to Lord Nigel?" asked Dreqnir.

Alamina felt a chill run through her. "I try not to think about it," she said. Then her expression brightened. "I have enough to think about, just planning for next semester!"

"I can help you with that," Alex said with a wink. "I dumped this place in your lap, and you've been doing wonderfully without me, but I spent so much time in the library while I was here, I never really got a chance to know the students. I'd like to do that in the few years I have left. You don't suppose there's an opening on the faculty for an old man with a talent for memorizing things?"

Alamina stood, walked around the desk, and kissed him lightly on the top of his head. "We're always looking for qualified instructors," she said, "and I can't think of anyone more qualified than you."

About the author

Stephen H. Provost is a novelist, historian, and journalist. During has worked for more than three decades as a managing editor, copy desk chief, columnist, and reporter at five newspapers. Now a full-time author, he has written on such diverse topics as American highways, dragons, mutant superheroes, mythic archetypes, language, department stores, and his hometown. He currently lives in Carson City, Nevada. And he loves cats. Read his blogs and keep up with his activities at stephenhprovost.com.

Did you enjoy this book?

Recommend it to a friend! And please consider rating it and/or leaving a brief review online at Amazon, Barnes & Noble and Goodreads.

Also by the author

Works of Fiction

Pathfinder of Destiny
Memortality (The Memortality Saga, 1)
Paralucidity (The Memortality Saga, 2)
The Only Dragon
Nightmare's Eve
Identity Break
Death's Doorstep
Feathercap

Works of Nonfiction

Yesterday's Highways
America's First Highways
Highway 99
Highway 101
Highways of the South
The Lincoln Highway in California
Victory Road
The Great American Shopping Experience
Mark Twain's Nevada
Martinsville Memories
Fresno Growing Up

The Talismans of Time

The Legend of Molly Bolin

A Whole Different League

Please Stop Saying That!

The Phoenix Principle

Media Meltdown

The Century Cities series:

Cambria Century, Carson City Century, Charleston Century, Danville Century, Fresno Century, Goldfield Century, Greensboro Century, Huntington Century, Roanoke Century, San Luis Obispo Century

Praise for other works

"The complex idea of mixing morality and mortality is a fresh twist on the human condition. ... **Memortality** is one of those books that will incite more questions than it answers. And for fandom, that's a good thing."

— Ricky L. Brown, Amazing Stories

"Punchy and fast paced, **Memortality** reads like a graphic novel. ... (Provost's) style makes the trippy landscapes and mind-bending plot points more believable and adds a thrilling edge to this vivid crossover fantasy."

— Foreword Reviews

"The genres in this volume span horror, fantasy, and science-fiction, and each is handled deftly. ... **Nightmare's Eve** should be on your reading list. The stories are at the intersection of nightmare and lucid dreaming, up ahead a signpost... next stop, your reading pile. Keep the nightlight on."

— R.B. Payne, Cemetery Dance

"**Memortality** by Stephen Provost is a highly original, thrilling novel unlike anything else out there."

— David McAfee, bestselling author of
33 A.D., 61 A.D., and 79 A.D.

"Profusely illustrated throughout, **Highway 99** is unreservedly recommended as an essential and core addition to every community and academic library's California History collections."

— California Bookwatch

"An essential primer for anyone seeking an entrée into the genre. Provost serves up a smorgasbord of highlights gleaned from his personal memories of and research into the various nooks and crannies of what 'used-to-be' in professional team sports."

— Tim Hanlon, Good Seats Still Available,
on **A Whole Different League**

"As informed and informative as it is entertaining and absorbing, **Fresno Growing Up** is very highly recommended for personal, community, and academic library 20th Century
American History collections."

— John Burroughs, Reviewer's Bookwatch

"Provost sticks mostly to the classics: vampires, ghosts, aliens, and even dragons. But trekking familiar terrain allows the author to subvert readers' expectations. ... Provost's poetry skillfully displays the same somber themes as the stories. ... Worthy tales that prove external forces are no more terrifying than what's inside people's heads."

— Kirkus Reviews on **Nightmare's Eve**

"...an engaging narrative that pulls the reader into the story and onto the road. ... I highly recommend **Highway 99: The History of California's Main Street**, whether you're a roadside archaeology nut or just someone who enjoys a ripping story peppered with vintage photographs."

— Barbara Gossett,
Society for Commercial Archaeology Journal

Made in the USA
Las Vegas, NV
24 January 2024

84800459R00194